Kiss of Death

THE HUSH SERIES

MARY ELIZABETH

Novels by the Author

Dusty Duet
Innocents (Dusty, Volume 1)
Delinquents (Dusty, Volume 2)

Closer Duet
Closer (Closer, Volume 1)
Sever (Closer, Volume 2)

Hush Series
Tramp (Hush, Volume 1)
Harlot (Hush, Volume 2)
Kiss of Death (Hush, Volume 2.5)
Criminal (Hush, Volume 3)
Vixen (Hush, Volume 4) Coming Soon

Standalone Novels
True Love Way
Low
Poesy (A Low Novella)
Extra Credit

For Janett.
Thank you.

Kiss of Death

One

RIP

Karma is a bitch.

No, really. Karma is a bitch.

And a dick tease.

"No touching, RIP." Karma wags her finger like she's a teacher reprimanding a naughty student and not a topless dancer in nothing but a pair of underwear scarcely covering her cunt. "You know the rules better than anyone."

"Which set of rules are we talking about?" I ask over the music. Sinking into my seat, I cross my arms over my chest to say, *happy now?* "Your rules? The clubs? Or—"

Her pretty mouth spreads into a condescending smirk as she straddles my lap, circling her hips. Needy hands slide up my biceps before she grips the tops of my shoulders and throws her head back, and I'm not complaining about the view. Neon lights dress the club in purples and blues, painting Karma's naked chest in sharp color as she moves over me in all the right motions. My cock hardens, turning Karma's condensation into conceit, and she grinds harder and faster.

A year ago, I would've bagged Karma and turned her out

in a back room without all the extra chitchat about rules and regulations before the song even ended.

Ironic, because a year ago, I didn't have a fraction of the power and influence in this city that was recently bestowed upon me after a quick vote and a drop of blood. My word went from a suggestion to law as soon as Nicolai Coppola placed this crown on my head. Instead of following orders, I'm the man dishing them out now. And everyone better do what the fuck I say or pay deadly consequences.

Unless you're a stripper with a knack for following protocol.

"Do I make you hard?" she asks, leaning forward to press her chest against my folded arms. "Do you want to fuck me?"

"Does it matter?" I ask in a bored tone.

This is supposed to be a celebration.

It's turned out to be nothing more than a reminder that my chosen family is going in the same direction as my cock.

Soft.

Karma flicks my earlobe with the tip of her tongue, grazing her fingernails across the back of my neck. Glitter dots her skin like diamonds, rubbing off on my shirt as she moves against me in what's turning out to be a run-of-the-mill private dance. She smells like strawberry candy, and I know from experience that she tastes like it, too.

"It's nothing personal." She works my arms apart to open me up by my wrists.

I roll my head to the side and say, "You're not acting like you don't want to be touched."

In a booth across the club, the DJ introduces the next dancer to take the stage. And as her music goes up, the lights turn down, blanketing us in shadows and a loose perception of privacy. Karma bends the rules in the dark, guiding her hands to her tits.

She's more than a handful, natural, round, with perfect fucking nipples that bead under my trace. With permission, I squeeze until my fingers overflow with her flesh, and she moans, thrusting faster to keep up with the beat of the music. The small cut on the tip of my finger stings, threatening to break open again. If blood spills, there won't be any vows of lifelong commitment this time. The only thing I'm after is a quick fuck with no strings attached.

I slide my hands around the small of her back, trapping her in my arms. "The risk is worth it."

Karma's long hair falls down her back to sweep across my knees as she bucks against me. She stops dancing for money to chase sensation, shuddering in my grasp—ignoring the fact that she's wrapped up with a killer. Sucking in a shaky breath like she's sucked my cock so many times before, a look of defiance darkens her eyes before she pulls her bottom lip between her teeth to taste rebellion.

Scanning the room for prying eyes, Karma's attention sweeps from one side of the club to the other. "Oh, god," she whimpers as I dip my head to capture her nipple in my mouth. "RIP..."

I smile with her nipple between my teeth, biting only hard enough to leave her gasping for more. Releasing her, I say, "Tell me to stop, and I'll stop."

"Don't stop." She clutches the lapels of my jacket, pressing our bodies together. "Fuck it. Fuck me."

Karma goes for my belt, releasing the leather strap from

the brass buckle with a swift flick of her wrist. Before power changed hands in our city, Grand Haven, and the touchable turned untouchable, we'd take this to a private room reserved for these kinds of arrangements between consenting adults. But there's a new queen in charge, and Lydia Montgomery has a monopoly on pussy from the Canadian border to Sacramento. Enemy territory is beyond that, smaller and weaker than us. And when the time comes, I have no doubt that with the help of the Coppolas, Lydia will stake her claim in the entire state.

Not only does Lydia run Hush, the largest high-end escort service in California, but she made a deal with the devil. What she says goes, and she says no one fucks for money without her permission. That includes me.

But she isn't the only one making deals with the dark side. The devil himself made me a made man, and that comes with a license to fuck who I want, when I want.

At least, it should. It used to mean absolute power.

A drink server walks past us, clearing their throat. "Karma, watch it," they say in passing, holding a tray of empty glasses.

The quick reminder of our debauchery is all it takes to break the spell, and Karma falls heavy in my arms with a sigh. We linger in a moment of dead space, stunned by the sudden jolt of disappointment before returning to our senses. My heartbeat doesn't slow with my breath but quickens with the urge to kill every motherfucker in the building before heading downtown to find Lydia. There's nothing I'd enjoy more than strangling the life out of that cockblocking bitch, even if a small part of me respects her reign.

"You know," Karma says in a sweet tone. She throws her arms over my shoulders lazily, swaying offbeat to the music.

The tops of her cheeks burn, and her eyes glaze in the semi-darkness. "How long have we shared this arrangement? We could be good together. It would be easy."

"Yeah?" I ask, only half invested. The plan tonight was to ride something, and if pussy is out of the question, then there's a black Harley Davidson waiting for me in the parking lot. I've wasted enough time here.

"Sure, why not? We're not so different."

A smile tugs at the corner of my mouth. "I don't even know your real name."

"I'm Amy."

Karma has a better ring to it.

"Do I need to sell myself?" she asks. "What else do you want to know?"

"Selling yourself is against the rules, remember?" I pat her thigh to signal the end of the dance, needing to get on the road before I combust.

Talk about a future together disappears with Amy's blush. People like us—the outliers—we're realists. We exist under the radar in dark corners, on whispers and secrets, where dreaming about a future could be the distraction that gets us killed. At the rate I'm going, the chances of living long enough to grow old, let alone with another person, are pointless.

Gangsters have a short life expectancy. The last don was killed at fifty years old, and the one before him wasn't much older. Same goes for the men who stood by their sides.

"It's nothing personal, Amy." I wink, repeating her words.

Using her real name is a mistake. It lifts the veil between fantasy and reality, transforming her from a product to a person. Amy isn't my wildest dream; she's a twentysomething girl wearing too much makeup to cover up the blanket of freckles laid across her nose and cheeks. The straps of her bra cut into her skin, and she winces as she stands. Amy's shoes are killing her feet.

"Don't I know it." She readies herself for the next sad son of a bitch who'll pay up for a dance leading nowhere, flattening her hands over her body. Amy nods toward the bar, correcting her hair, and asks, "The shelves were made of glass, and there used to be a mirror behind the liquor. It gave an illusion that the bar was bigger than it actually is."

Complacency could be the last thing I do. With as many enemies as I have, I notice everything. When I step into a space, the first thing I do is look for a way out and check for suspicious behavior. Nothing gets past me, and I noted the liquor bottles were situated on the countertop and the normal liquor display was gone when I arrived. It's in the process of being rebuilt, so I wrote it off as the result of a bar fight, looks like I was wrong.

"What happened?" I ask.

"Chasity gave a customer a hand job in the bathroom, and it got back to Hush."

Standing to my feet, I pull my shirt straight and shake my head. Lydia has the entire mob at her disposal, but I've heard stories about how she deals with those who break the rules. It involves a nightstick and quality swing.

"She walked right through the doors last week like she owned the place. Tommy tried to explain. He tried to calm her down, but it went in one ear and out the other." Amy chuckles softly, with an edge of admiration in the tone. "No woman in history has ever calmed down when a man has asked her to.

Not that Lydia needed to calm down at all. She was as cold as ice, stopping him in his tracks with a single look. Nothing was left untouched. The liquor bottles, the mirrors, the shelves, and every glass in sight was gone in a matter of seconds."

That's why I work with guns.

When I wave a weapon around, people usually shut the fuck up and do as they're told without the mess of breaking shit.

When I fire my pistol, it's clean shots only.

It's easier to cover up a crime scene that way. And quicker.

"Before she left," Amy continues. She pinches her cheeks and runs a finger under her bottom lip for smeared lipstick. "Lydia pointed the stick at Chasity and said, *you're better than a cheap fuck in the bathroom stall,* and the poor girl burst into tears. Tommy fired her, of course. That fifty-dollar hand job cost him a hundred grand. So, as much as I'd like to fuck you, RIP, I don't want to lose my job. I'm going places."

"Let me guess," I say, opening my jacket to adjust my gun holster. Twin Glocks hug my left and right sides, fully loaded. Always ready to play. "You're paying your way through college."

A smile breaks her face in half, but it doesn't reach her eyes. Amy dips her toe in this life, dancing for gangsters and selling her body when allowed. But she knows when she's out of her league.

"Now why would I do something like that?" She takes an unconscious step back. "I stand to make more money with Hush than I ever could with a college degree. And in a shorter amount of time."

"What do you mean with Hush?"

The music changes again, and the stage goes dark as the

lights in the club transition from purple and blue to neon pink and yellow. Amy doesn't know me outside of our arrangements, but she's heard stories. Stories she's likely visualizing now. Unease chips away at her the longer we stand under the warmer lights, harsh tones cutting shadows across my face. Her eyes wander, but no one turns their back on the most dangerous man in the building.

Fuck me for a few hundred dollars? Yes.

But have a conversation with me? That's pushing it.

"Isn't it obvious?" She only manages to make eye contact for fleeting moments. Self-preservation is an uneasy pull in the pit of her stomach. *Danger*, it warns her. *Danger*. Amy hides it well, motioning around the club like I'm a normal patron— like most of the men in attendance tonight don't work for me. "A gentlemen's club is the perfect place to find quality girls. If we do well enough here, we're promoted. And the pay raise is worth axing bathroom hand jobs."

Now it makes sense. This isn't only a strip joint; it's a fucking pussy farm. And Lydia doesn't want anyone sampling the goods before she gets her hands on them first.

Pulling my wallet from my back pocket, I thumb through the bills and pay Amy the going rate before Lydia interfered with our arrangement.

"RIP," she says hesitantly. "This is too much money. It was only a dance."

I don't miss the way Amy inhales a sharp breath as I lean in to press a small kiss to her forehead. This woman was ready to let me inside her body, but without the illusion of a business transaction between us, she senses what everyone does when I'm around: fear.

"It was a great dance," I say. "Take care of yourself, Amy."

"Wait," she calls out over the music, making no attempt to follow me out. "If you change your mind and decide you're ready for a girlfriend, you know where to find me."

"You got it, babe." I wink and head to the bar, where my guys are gathered.

Not a chance. What the fuck would I do with a girlfriend?

The Coppola crime family took me under their wing at a young age. I was a gutter kid, running the streets so I didn't have to face my alcoholic mother and abusive father at home more than necessary. Gino Coppola, who was the underboss, caught me stealing a pack of gum from a liquor store protected by the organization. He beat my ass, but then he gave me a job. Gino was dead in a year, but my association with the Coppolas didn't die with him.

The work started off small. I delivered messages, eavesdropped, cleaned up around various hangouts, and kept the boss's grandson, Nicolai, company. But as I grew, so did my responsibilities. It turned out that I was light on my feet and really fucking good with a gun.

During my association, I've survived the death of two bosses, two underbosses, and countless soldiers, but I didn't bat a fucking eye when Nico voted me in. La Costa Nostra is what I know. I live by the gun, and one day, I'll likely die by that motherfucker. Where does that leave room for a girlfriend? Where does something as trivial as a relationship fit? It doesn't.

On my way to the top, I've run through my fair share of women. Sex isn't a problem. My face, my build, my bike and even my reputation brings them in. Girls outside the life think they want a bad boy until things get bad. Then they get scared and run. On the rare occasion when someone sticks around, determined to "fix me", I lose interest and send them on their way.

A Mafia princess has grown up in the lifestyle, so I don't have to live a double life like I do with a normal woman. But there's nothing casual about hooking up with a made man's little girl, even if she's a twenty-three-year-old cookie who likes her mouth fucked. Their only concern is marrying her off to an honorable man to become his problem, even if that man is a killer.

I'm not looking that far ahead.

I don't connect with people.

I tolerate them, or I kill them.

The general disconnection I have for others may be a result of growing up in a loveless home. Doctors have labeled me as "detached" and "compulsive" while scribbling prescriptions, promising a cure. But my loyalties lie only with those who've proven to have my back, and there're only a few individuals I trust. Everyone in my life has a role and serves a purpose, and when that role or purpose expires, so do they. Be it I send them away or put them in the grave.

And I don't feel guilty about it.

Except once.

My first kill was the only time I hesitated before pulling the trigger, and it's my only experience with regret. The memory still keeps me up at night.

But ghosting a woman? Good riddance.

I can't be fixed. There's no point in letting anyone try.

The day will come when I'm expected to marry, likely to a *principessa,* who'll want my status but not my heart. Which works because I don't have one. Until then, I don't mind I'll pay for what I need, when I need it.

Anyone who says they're too good to pay for sex is lying.

There's only one thing I hate more than Lydia Montgomery's new rules, and that's a liar.

Two

RIP

Trinity Gentlemen's Club is as good as it gets.

The atmosphere, the crowd, the bar—before it was destroyed—and the girls are the best California has to offer. It's exclusive, high end, and caters to the underbelly taking over Grand Haven.

And I'm absolutely fucking bored with the entire thing.

"I'm out of here." I clap my top capo, Frank Russel, on the shoulder. "We'll catch up tomorrow."

He spins his barstool around, holding a glass of liquor in one hand and pushing his hair out of his face with the other. Frank, *The Damage*, as the rest of the city calls him, smiles unbothered. Dark liquid swirls in his glass as he holds it out to me in salute. "Not fucking happening, Rip," he says. "We just got here. Sit your ass down and have a drink."

Nodding toward the five or six men gathered around the bar collecting dozens of empty shot glasses in front of them, I say, "Make sure they keep their hands to themselves, would you? I don't need those kinds of problems right now."

Frank lets out a small chuckle. "Yeah, we heard about the

new rules. We have some shit lined up, and money won't be exchanged. We're all good here."

"Nice to hear. You guys have a good time tonight." I drop a couple hundred dollars on the bar to pay for their next round and retreat. "We have that shipment to handle at the docks tomorrow. Be there. Sober."

"Oh, no you don't," Damage calls out. He jumps from his stool and jogs after me before I make it out the door, capturing my wrist to pull me back. "This is a fucking party, and you're the guest of honor."

Men in this business tend to steer clear from me unless absolutely necessary, but Frank isn't afraid to bust my balls on a regular basis.

"You think you're scary because you have a gun?" he asked me once. *"Well, I got a gun too."*

I drew the line when he asked me to be the best man at his wedding last summer, but Frank is one of the few people I trust. He's the closest thing a guy like me in a life like this has to a friend. Being around him doesn't make my trigger finger twitch. Normally.

Pushing me onto an empty barstool, Frank claps his palm on the counter and says, "Can we get this man a Coca-Cola? None of that Pepsi shit," he makes clear. "We want the good, good soda. We're celebrating Rip's promotion. Only the best will do."

I can't help the smile on my face. "One drink. I'll have one drink and then I'm out."

Frank stares with distaste at the frosted glass of Coke our bartender slides in front of me, and he pretends to pour liquor from his glass into mine. "Just a little will make your night a whole lot better. You need to loosen up."

This type of behavior doesn't warrant a response. He knows, and I know, that I'm the last person to succumb to peer pressure. Frank's free to spike my drink, but he's not free from the consequences of his decisions. Damage is one of my only friends, but my interpretation of friendship is loose. People tend to bargain for their lives when staring down the barrel of a gun, and friends are always first on the chopping block.

I've seen it again and again. In the end, friendship doesn't mean much.

"That'll kill you," Frank says. He nods toward my Coke. "People use that shit to erode battery acid from car engines. Stuff like that shouldn't go into a human body."

"We're all going to die," I remind him, spinning around toward the stage as the lights go down. "And it won't be from anything we eat or drink."

"I'll toast to that," he mumbles.

Rick Ross's "Hustlin'" plays from the sound system, and the stage goes completely dark as the bass goes all the way up. The beat from the music fills the empty space inside of my chest where a heart should be, pulsating within my bones, pounding behind my eyes and in my teeth. My men make their way to the front for an up close and personal experience, taking their drinks and ruckus with them. Frank and I hang back, preferring our view from here.

"Word is this next girl is good," Frank says conversationally.

"Who is she?" I ask.

"Newbie." He shakes his empty glass at the bartender

for a refill. "Started sometime last week. Name is Vera. Vera Monroe."

In a club called Trinity, with dancers named Karma, Chasity, Cherry, Trixie and whoever the fuck else, Vera sounds misplaced. But Monroe tugs on something at the back of my mind, and I can't place it no matter how many times I turn the name over.

Monroe.

Monroe.

Monroe.

"Frank, do we know a Mon…" Contemplating the name, I turn toward my soda when the lights in the entire club go out. Without sight, my other senses intensify. Music is deeper and conversation carries higher. I can taste the aroma of Frank's bitter liquor in the air and feel the warmth of blood in my veins, in direct contrast to how cold the mug is in my hand.

Instinctively, I tune it all out and narrow down on my surroundings, listening for sudden movement, open doors, or a bullet loading into a chamber. I can't see a thing, but I remember where every person in the club is standing, where the exits are, and my weapons are heavy at my sides—locked and loaded.

"Relax," Frank says. "It's part of the show."

Cool condensation drips over my fingers. "Ballsy to leave a bunch of wise guys in the dark."

The hum of excited voices breaks as the lights above the stage glow red, illuminating the platform. Artificial fog acts as a wall between us and the show, slowly dissipating to reveal the silhouette of a girl … *no*, a woman … lying at the front of the stage with her back curved and knees up, showcasing a perfect hourglass figure. My eyes follow her small waist down to a round bottom, thick thighs, and long legs that lead to a pair of tall platform heels.

The dancer stretches her arms above her head, elongating her flat stomach and pushing her chest out to emphasize the size of her tits. Dropping her head back, she drags her hands down the curve of her slender neck over her breasts. The group gathered around the stage cheers, tossing dollar bills as she opens her thighs and circles her hips like an open invitation to fuck.

She's a shadow, a red-light special, casting a spell and bringing the entire club to a standstill. The other dancers wish they were her, while the spectators wish they were inside of her. Even me. I palm the back of my neck as my cock swells, clearing my throat before I do something embarrassing like groan with pent-up frustration.

"Goddamn!" Frank calls out, backhanding my chest as the woman on stage rises on all fours. She crawls toward the pole in languid strides, giving us a good look at what it would be like to take her from behind. "It doesn't get better than this."

With one hand on the pole, she pulls herself up and walks in circles. Slow at first, she picks up speed as the music crescendos, building and building and building like the pressure in my chest. When the beat finally drops and I exhale a large breath, she swings her legs up to catch the pole between her knees in a crucifix pose. The people closest to the stage erupt, and it's all I can do not to put a fucking bullet in their heads.

She calls to me.

Maybe the crimson light on her skin calls to me like blood calls to me.

Maybe it's because as the shadows disappear, the severity in her stare looks like my own.

Or maybe it's because she can work a pole like a motherfucking dream.

But she calls to me.

She's a siren before a tornado.

A warning.

A vixen.

Vera hooks one knee around the steel rod while extending her second leg out, leaning straight back. Her long black hair flies like a cape as she rotates around the stripper pole, untying her top with a flick of her wrist. Satin and lace slip from her fingers and fall to the stage like a feather, cascading back and forth before landing gently on a blanket of cash. I push away from my seat, licking my lips at the sight of her naked breasts. And as I approach the stage, busy excitement from my men and the heavy beats rumbling from the sound system drop to muted echoes. There could be a gun pointed at the back of my head, and I wouldn't hear the shot.

Something takes hold of me, drawing me forward. I don't push through the audience. I grab the closest person within reach by the back of their neck and shove them away, and the others quickly scatter. I haven't been a shot caller for long and throwing around my weight for the sake of getting my way isn't my style, but my reputation proceeds me. It speaks for itself and comes through in a clutch.

Move.

Or I'll fucking remove you for good.

I drag a chair to the front of the stage and take a seat, leaning back with my knees apart. The pole is an extension of her body in the same way as my guns are an extension of myself, and the severity in our stares isn't the only thing we have in common. We're craftsmen, natural in our ability to command a room. Vera's dance isn't only to get my dick hard. She's a magician, and I'm hypnotized. No request is too small. If she asked me to jump on one leg and pat the top of my head, I'm jumping on one leg and patting the top of my fucking head.

Luckily, she only wants me to open my wallet.

Reaching inside my jacket pocket, I grab a stack of cash and break the band to make it rain. Hundred-dollar bills fall onstage like bread crumbs in the forest, but if I have anything to do with it, she'll never find her way home. My castle isn't built with candy, but skulls and bones. She's taunted that bad guy, and I'll throw us both in the fire before she gets away.

Sliding down the pole with her legs in the splits, she lands lightly on her feet with a devious glint in her eyes. Vera pushes the money around with the toe of her platform before sauntering over, waving her hips from side to side. Cash mutes her footsteps, but her presence is loud and turns the heat up. She kneels in front of me, fingertips dancing on her knees, and I pull my collar from my neck as a bead of sweat drips down my spine.

"Enjoying the show?" she asks, parting her thighs to give me an uninterrupted view of her lace-covered pussy. Vera rolls her hips. "I sure hope so, because you've scared everyone else off."

Revealing another band of hundreds, I say, "I'm all you need, baby."

Dropping her head back, Vera laughs out loud. The sound

catches a spark under my skin, and I'd gladly drain my bank account to hear it again.

"Be careful what you wish for." Vera runs a finger down between her breasts, lower, lower … lower past her belly toward her pelvis. She slips a fingertip under the waistband of her lace thong, sliding it from hip to hip suggestively. "You just might get it."

My cock strains against my fly, rock hard and eager to be fucked or fisted. A bead of moisture seeps at the swollen tip, and I don't need to see it to know the veins running up and down the shaft are engorged with blood. As the tension in my stomach becomes overwhelming, I shift in my seat and adjust the fit of my jeans, looking for relief. It only worsens.

Vera pulls her bottom lip between her teeth and smiles flirtatiously, eyeing the cause of my dilemma like a snack. She stands to her feet, stomach tight and nipples hard, playing with the idea of removing her panties. Looking down at me, she lowers the lace on one side of her hip before pulling it up and bringing it down on the other, teetering back and forth in a *should I* or *shouldn't I* motion.

Just when I think she might pull them off, the song ends, and her set is over. I sit forward to rest my elbows on my knees, watching her retreat with a growl trapped in my throat. Vera reaches down for her top as she goes, shaking it free from cash caught in the straps. She doesn't bother to gather the money herself, disappearing behind the curtain with a lingering look at me over her shoulder. An employee appears with a push broom, sweeping her earnings into piles. I throw the stack of cash in my hand on top and get up.

"You're going to New York to meet The Ruin, aren't you?" Frank asks when I return to the bar.

The Ruin, now a syndicate of the highest-ranked gangsters in the United States, meet up when ranks among the organizations change hands. I am The Ruin now, and Nicolai and I are flying to the East Coast next week to formally introduce ourselves. We're self-governed, but accountability keeps us from killing each other to extension and mowing down the entire country. Want to order a hit on a rival don? Ask The Ruin. Want to run guns, drugs, or women through someone else's territory? Ask The Ruin. Break the rules, and deal with The Ruin.

"Get the green light and take out that Montgomery broad," he says half jokingly. "Then you can have any woman without asking for permission like some fucking sucker."

I throw more money on the bar to pay for my soda before picking it up to drink it in a single swallow. The ice has melted, sitting atop the syrup and watering down the carbonation. Fizz tickles the back of my throat as it goes down, and my eyes water against the sting. Lowering my glass to the countertop, I wipe my mouth on the back of my hand and pat Frank on the shoulder. His suggestion doesn't warrant a response.

"See you in the morning, boss," he calls after me.

This marks the first time anyone has called me boss since making my vows to the Coppola outfit. A smile curves my lips as I leave, stopping just outside the door to inhale a deep breath. Grand Haven is rotten at the core, but it's hard not to appreciate the scenery. The Pacific Ocean rages just across the street, a void under the cloud-covered night. Cool air bites my overheated skin, salt kisses my lips, and the white-capped waves crashing on shore whisper the many ways she'd tear me apart if I dared to touch her in her sweetest tone.

My bike, a Harley Davidson Street Glide Special, is parked up front. If my heart is capable of loving anything at all, then this is the love of my life. Lights from the club's marquee shine in the gloss-black finish, twinkling from fender to fender. The sight of my motorcycle turns the curl tugging at the corner of my mouth into a complete smile. I shake tension from my arms as I approach it, letting go of everything but the anticipation of climbing on and starting the engine.

"I know who you are," a voice battling the sea for romantic barbarity calls to me from behind.

"If that was true, you wouldn't have snuck up on me," I say. A chill runs through my arms, and it's not because of my Harley.

The soft scent of peach and jasmine mingles with the salty air as she walks by and steps off the curb to my bike. Dressed in ripped jeans, a white tee, and a leather jacket similar to my own, Vera glides her finger down the length of the gas tank to the leather seat. I ball my hands to keep from reaching out and touching her waist-length hair, dark as the midnight sky. But also to keep from wrapping my hand around it at the root and pulling.

"Girls whisper about you in the dressing room between sets." She leans against my bike and crosses her ankles. If she's afraid of me, she's doing a good job hiding it. "You're RIP. Alessi. Mafia hit man. The streets call you as *Rest in Peace.*"

Stretching, twisting, and rolling her body under the red lights, Vera looked six feet tall. Face to face, she stands a little more than five feet, but the girl has a huge set of balls for coming at me like this. If she were anyone less beautiful and curious, those would be her last words. She needs to proceed with caution, or they still may be.

"What Mafia?" I ask, fascinated by her boldness. Stepping down from the curb, I slide my hands into my pockets, circling her like a lion circles its target before a kill. "Look around, babe. Grand Haven is squeaky fucking clean."

Shrugging, Vera's violet eyes follow me as I stroll past her. "That depends on what side of the line you're on."

No one stands with their back to me on purpose. But I'm surprised as I come around to the other side of the bike and she doesn't spin to face me. Vera lifts her face to the night sky and sighs, her warm breath turning to clouds in the cool air.

"Are you going to tell me your name then?" she asks. "Since I have it all wrong."

I close the space between us and loom over her, leaving only inches between my chest and her back. Vera draws in a sharp breath at my nearness, and her shoulders lift as she breathes, small and breakable. But she shows no signs of real self-preservation. When she should be running from my touch, she remains still as I rub the ends of her hair between my fingers. It would be so easy to sink my teeth into her, eating her up like a meal.

"My mother named me Rip. The rest is made-up bullshit."

My name is Rip. Not RIP.

The moniker is convenient, ironic, and only a coincidence. Who knows, maybe my parents sensed that I was born up to no good and labeled me appropriately. They may have looked each other in the eyes on the day I was delivered and said,

*"This boy will grow up to be a killer. Let's give the media some-
thing they can play with."*

No one calls me *Rest in Peace* to my face. It's all implica-
tion. But my parents were onto something. I'm twenty-eight
years old and have yet to face a murder charge, but the media
loves the RIP headlines when I so much as cop a speeding
ticket.

She turns her head to the side, and I let go of her hair.
"So, you're not a Mafia hit man."

Chucking, I answer, "No, I'm not."

Not anymore.

I'm much worse than that now.

"I don't buy that. You're definitely someone." Turning
around, she places her hands on the seat and leans forward to
check me out. Nodding toward my black Doc Martens, and
then to the visible tattoos covering my hand and neck, she says,
"You look more like a biker than an underworld king."

Lifting my chin, I square my shoulders and stare down at
her. "Who the fuck are you?"

"Vera Monroe."

"You ask a lot of fucking questions, Vera Monroe." Again,
the name pulls on a long-forgotten memory.

I didn't confirm her suspicions, but she's standing in the
shadow of a menace and knows it. Pulling her bottom lip between her teeth, she chews on it, not with alarm, but like she's
trying to force two wrong puzzle pieces together. They look
like a good fit, but something is off. On the outside, I look like
a man. My face is symmetrical. I have a strong jaw, piercing
brown eyes, and everything about me screams absolute, un-
diluted masculinity. But my presence makes her bones hurt,

and she doesn't know why. But no one ever puts a pretty face on a nightmare.

Before she can see me clearly, Vera squints against a pair of headlights that streak across her face. She holds her hand against the light until the black SUV pulls all the way up, parking in front of the club. The windows are blacked out, and the license plate is confidential. I expect some high roller to get out, but Vera pushes away from my bike.

"That's my ride," she says with a regretful smile. "Maybe I'll see you around, Rip Alessi, not a Mafia hit man."

"Is that your boyfriend or something?"

"No, it's an Uber."

"I've never seen an Uber like that."

Backing away, she winks. "It's a luxury Uber. I had a lucrative night."

Swinging a leg over my bike, I sit back and start the engine. The rumble fractures the night. "Fuck that. Get on."

Three

RIP

An older black man with a headful of white hair beneath a driving cap exits the Suburban, limping with a pained knee. He pulls his cuffs straight and motions to the back door as if to open it for Vera. I've never taken a fucking Uber in my life, but even I know they don't come with confidential plates and a chauffeur.

Pushing the kickstand up, I hold the bike straight between my legs and back it out of the parking spot. Vera watches, hesitating between her ride and the Harley.

Red pill. Blue pill.

"I don't have a helmet," she says over the roar of the engine.

"Wear mine." I flip the headlamp on, dousing her in white light, and open the left saddlebag. Holding my helmet up, I say, "Get on the bike. I'm taking you home."

"That's not necessary."

I hang the helmet from the handlebars and park my ass, crossing my arms over my chest to wait this out. If she tries to walk away from me, I'll drag her back. If the driver of the

SUV tries to stop me, his knee will be the least of his prob-lems. There's no scenario where she doesn't end up on my bike.

Filling her lungs with air, she dismisses the driver with a swift wave of her hand and concedes with a heavy exhale. She swipes the helmet and places it on her head, attempt-ing to secure the strap beneath her chin alone. Between the power under my legs and the amusement I feel watching her fumble with the buckle, parts of myself I thought dead spark with signs of life. Shaking my head, I smile with the unfa-miliar lightness in my chest.

"Enjoying yourself?" she asks, pressing her tongue to the corner of her mouth. Pushing her hands away, I pull the strap tight before securing it in place. "Take me straight home, Rip. I have an appointment in the morning that I can't miss."

"I make no promises."

Taking a step back, she jabs her thumb over her shoul-der. "Then I'm going with him."

A flash of irritation warms the palms of my hands, and I clear my throat before I say something that ruins our night. Gun handles peek out from beneath my jacket, a so-bering reminder of who the fuck I am, but I tuck them away before I do something that ruins lives. What's stopping me from shooting the driver to take away her options? She can run, but I'm faster. She can fight, but I'm stronger.

Shaking the thought from my head, I hook my arm around her waist and pull her close. "You don't want to go with him. I excite you. My bike excites you. Get on and let's go. I'll get you home at a decent hour."

"It's after midnight. We're past decent." She mounts the

bike, and the toes of her Converse skid the pavement as she struggles to find her footing. Her warm breath caresses the back of my neck as she leans forward to say, "This is new to me. Am I doing it right?"

"Is this your first time on a motorcycle?" I question over my shoulder. The inside of her knees brush against the outside of my legs, and she squeezes to hold me tight, trembling with nervousness.

"Please, don't kill me." Vera wraps her arms around my middle.

Dropping my head back, I laugh out loud, unable to help myself. Thirty minutes ago, she defied gravity in a pair of ankle-breaking platforms on stage in front of a group of wise guys who'd love nothing more than to break her apart, and she didn't so much as flinch. I find it incredibly fucking amusing that riding on the back of my motorcycle scares her more than that.

How many times has someone begged me not to kill them? Dozens of times? Hundreds? A couple hundred?

It falls on deaf ears. If you find yourself face to face with me, you're already dead. It's just a matter of semantics at that point. But no one has ever asked me to spare their life in this context, and I've never wanted to keep someone breathing more than I do now.

"You're safe." I peel her fingers from my jacket and secure her arms all the way around me. Anticipation warms my face as she fists my T-shirt right above my waist and buries her face in my neck, smiling against my heated skin. "Hold me tight. Don't let go."

The engine's rumble explodes into a roar that stretches

across the night like a shock wave, silencing the ocean and everything around it. We absorb the vibration beneath the leather seat, trembling with the power between our legs. Wide awake, every nerve ending in our bodies fires up as adrenaline doses our bloodstreams—a rush that will intensify the faster we go.

"Oh, I like that," she whispers. Her lips brush against the shell of my ear. "Do it again."

"Be careful what you wish for," I repeat her words from earlier and drop the bike into gear.

Frank and our crew exit the club just as the white-haired driver plucks the cap from his head and twists it in his hands. Vera's would-be chauffeur watches anxiously when we pull out of the parking lot onto the main highway, but Frank and the rest of our guys holler and whistle as we disappear down the road. Their praise never meets my ears, but I know they'll be full of questions tomorrow.

The bike races through first gear, to second, to third gear, and fourth. Vera's grip on my shirt tightens, but the wind soothes her, caressing her face and sliding around the back of her neck to lift the hair from her shoulders in a moment of absolute weightlessness. I watch her in the side mirrors as the broken lines in the road blur into a single streak of yellow right down the middle.

"Open your eyes," I say, heading down a stretch of highway that leads to the heart of the city.

We approach a police cruiser with a radar gun sticking out from the window. We're over the forty-five-mile-per-hour speed limit, but my bigger offense is operating a motorcycle without a helmet. I make eye contact with the patrol person as we pass, the wind moving through my hair, unsure if this particular officer is on our payroll or not. If they pull me over, there's going to be a problem. I'm not ready to end my night with Vera just yet.

The officer shakes their head as we go, ignoring civil duty to collect on the fat stack of cash the syndicate passes down each month to buy an extra layer of protection from the law.

"My apartment is the other way," Vera says. Her death grip loosens as she relaxes, daring to lift her face from my jacket to look around. She glances at the grin on my face and says, "You're not even sorry, are you?"

"Not even a little."

The ocean passes on our left, sea spray dancing under the orange glow of the streetlights, while the buildings on our right grow in size the closer we get to Main Street. On the outside, Grand Haven, California, pretends to be another tech city within reach of Silicon Valley. We've raised the rent, pushed out the poor, and shut down old mom-and-pop joints to turn them into commercial coffee shops and art galleries no one really gives a fuck about. We cater to the rich, the up-and-comer, and the next big thing.

It's a ruse.

Grand Haven is a jungle gym for organized crime. Our hands are in everything from waste management, art trade, and imports and exports that come and go from port every day. The mob has come a long way from days of shelling banned liquor from dirty warehouses. We set up shop in the tallest high-rise in the city now.

"Where are you taking me?" Vera asks.

"There's something I want to show you."

We race past the marina, where fishing vessels are lit up as they unload their catch in time for the fresh fish market in the morning. Seagulls circle the boats for their chance to nick a meal, squawking over the rumble of the engine, and seals bark from the water.

The harbor quickly turns into the art district, the shopping district, and finally, the financial district. High-rise buildings reach for the sky like titans, one after another, mostly dark and lying in wait for an early morning jump at world domination. I slow down as we come up to the tallest of them all, right in the center of Grand Haven, a massive structure that reflects the ocean and the heavens in a mirror finish. When I notice a vehicle parked out front, I pull to the shoulder about a block away.

"We live near the most beautiful beaches in California, and you bring me here?" Vera asks with a small laugh. "I didn't take you as the romantic type, but this is…"

I give her a quick look over my shoulder. The tip of her nose is red, and her eyes are glassy under the streetlight. As hard as it is to look away from her windblown expression, I turn and nod toward the Ridge & Sons building. "We're going there."

Vera removes the helmet and shakes her hair free, squeezing me with her knees to keep straight on the bike. Heat pools in the pit of my stomach, and it's all I can do not to pull her on my lap. Slip my hand under her shirt. Taste her lips. Feel her from the inside.

"Do you have business with the good lawyers?" she asks, leaning forward to rest her chin on my shoulder. It's a gesture normally shared between familiars, not two people who've just met. But it doesn't bother me. The fact that it doesn't should. She asks, "How would we even get inside a place like that at this time?"

Planting my boots on the road, I hold the bike up and cross my arms over my chest. The white Lamborghini Huracan parked in front of the Ridge & Sons high-rise suddenly fires, cracking like thunder. Bright LED lights illuminate the street like spotlights, crisp and white. A prism of color reflecting from the wall of mirrors is interrupted when the building's front entrance opens, and two people emerge.

"There she is," Vera says in a smooth tone. She presses herself against my back, circling her arms back around me. "That's the baddest bitch in town."

After what I saw Vera do on stage tonight, I doubt it.

But Lydia Montgomery has a reputation that beats my own for notoriety.

Sleek.

That woman is sleek.

The word crosses my tongue as she steps into the light, but I cage it behind my teeth. Everyone on this side of good and evil knows Lydia, but she's the kind of woman who makes you feel like you're seeing her for the first time, every time. Tall, pristine, and razor sharp, the world comes to a standstill in her presence. Because most of all, she's powerful.

"Between you and me," Vera says, flattening her palms against my stomach to hold me closer. "I think she's doing it all wrong."

Turning my head, we come nose to nose. "Doing what wrong?"

Violet eyes meet mine long enough for the tension between us to become palpable, and then she lowers them to my lips. "All of it," she says.

"Lydia, get in the damn car," a male says in a voice loud enough to carry down the street.

Talent Ridge. Youngest of the Ridge brothers. Double fucking agents.

Guilt is an itch at the back of my throat. It's an ache in my joints. A crease between my eyebrows. Talent is a constant reminder that despite our history and the stakes we share in each other's lives now, what's already been done can't be undone. Ever.

Cradling Lydia's face in his hands, Talent bends at the knees to look her in the eyes. He doesn't get the reaction he was hoping for and pushes away, circling around the car to the driver's side with his hands in his hair. Talent is intense. She's stoic. And I don't know how he fell in love with her. It must be like sticking your dick in a great white shark and hoping she doesn't eat your fucking heart out.

"Must be trouble in paradise." Vera sighs as the car races away. With no one in sight, she climbs off the bike and smooths down her hair. "Are we breaking in or what?"

After a short walk, I enter the service elevator's access code inside the Ridge & Sons parking garage.

Vera bounces from foot to foot, exhaling warm breath into her hands as we wait for the elevator cab to arrive. "Our definitions of breaking and entering are very different, Rip. I was looking forward to breaking one of those pretty windows out front and ransacking the place. But you practically have the keys to the castle."

Our lift arrives with a ding, and I step aside to allow her in first. "Let's leave the law out of this. We have a rocky relationship."

"Can't imagine why," she teases.

How the fuck did I end up in the Ridge & Sons service elevator with a stripper?

Ankles crossed, Vera leans on the rail across from me. She isn't afraid to meet my stare, even if she is the first to look away, distracted by my mouth. Nothing was confirmed, but my identity is no well-kept secret, and she still willingly trapped herself inside a box with a professional hit man. Someone on the straight and narrow knows better than that. When they realize the cute guy with an edge is an actual criminal, they run. Vera only points to a silent speaker in the corner and says, "Kind of weird without the classical music."

She's harder than some naive girl. It's practiced resilience that could have been learned by dancing for gangsters at Trinity, but Frank said she was new. And I'm not convinced Vera's Mafia-born. Those girls would be offended I'd offered them a ride on my motorcycle instead of a car like Talent's. They're mouthy, stuck up, and bored.

But I'd know if she was attached to the family. I've lived in the area most of my life, and someone like Vera doesn't go unnoticed.

"Where are you from?" I ask, breaking the silence.

"California."

"Where in California? It's a big fucking state."

Tilting her head to the side, she narrows her eyes and asks, "Why?"

"Is Monroe your real name?" I lick my lips. She doesn't have to tell me where she's from. This is the twenty-first fucking century, and we have the internet. Nothing is a secret.

"I have nothing to hide from you." Stepping away from the elevator wall, she pirouettes. Her black hair fans around her in the spin before she comes to a stop directly in front of me. "You don't scare me. That look in your eyes doesn't scare me. Your guns don't scare me."

"Why not?"

Clutching the lapels of my jacket, she rises onto the tips of her shoes and whispers, "I know you."

She evades my reach when the doors part, stepping onto the roof of the highest building in Northern California. The wind captures her hair, swirling it around her head before dumping it back over her shoulders the farther she steps away from the elevator. The temperature is low ground level, but that feels like summer heat compared to how cold it is this close to the moon.

Jasmine and peach lure me from the elevator cab, where the fragrance drifts in the frigid air. I press my burning lips together and close my eyes, inhaling like a predator catching the scent of their prey. The pulse point in my neck throbs, pumping blood into my muscles. My shoulders square up, biceps flex, and my feet move me through the shadows until I'm ready to strike.

As innocent as a doe in the woods, Vera looks over her shoulder with bright red cheeks and wide, glassy eyes. She's unhurt by the cold, teeth chattering under a smile. I pull the collar of my shirt away from my neck, burning alive. If

I were a gentleman in the right state of mind, I'd offer my jacket to wear on top of her own. But when her lips move, I don't hear a word over the sound of my heart echoing through my ears. It grows louder and louder as adrenaline kicks in and logic fucks off.

Stupid girl.

Stupid fucking bitch.

I step into the light.

And she climbs onto the ledge of the roof.

"Would I die before I hit the ground?" She glances over the side of the building, contemplating the long fall. "Or is that a myth?"

Sound returns in a rush, and cool air burns my lungs as I inhale a sharp breath. "Get down."

The clouds have disappeared on a breeze, revealing a thick blanket of stars that blurs with the city lights on the horizon—a backdrop to her performance. Vera tiptoes on the edge of the building, carefully testing her footing before taking bigger steps.

"Would I?" she asks again, holding her hands out to stabilize herself. "Do assassins bother with fun facts like that, or are you the type to just point and shoot?"

Swallowing around the lump in my throat, I hold my hand out. "Vera…"

"Is it something you can switch on and off?" She opens her chest, stretching her arms above her head and posing her hands to make a perfect circle. "Did you know your eyes change when you're about to kill someone? That is what was about to happen before I climbed up here, right? Did I ask too many questions? Pry? Do I scare you more than you scare me?"

Distress strangles me, and I choke, coughing to clear my airway.

"I taught myself how to dance." Sliding her foot forward, she circles it around. Vera spins, opening her arms, and spins again, closing them. "Anyone with good balance and upper body strength can pole dance. Ballet is totally different. Ballerinas are born, not made. I have natural talent, but I'm too mean to dance competitively. I'd first slit someone's throat than fight for a spot in the show. I want it all."

She keeps her back straight and starts in a lunge, pressing her hands to the top of the ledge. Kicking her feet over her head, Vera holds her legs in the splits before landing the cartwheel with her back toward me.

"Fuck," I breathe out, taking another step forward.

"I'm decent, though." A strand of hair blows across her face as she looks over her shoulder. "Good enough to get your attention."

"You had everyone's attention." I've never been more aware of my own heartbeat than I am now. The pounding in my throat expands to my elbows, my wrists, knees, and ankles, driving blood through my veins. It's everywhere and nowhere all at once.

She shrugs. "What about you, Rip? Were you born or made to kill?"

"Both," I answer honestly.

Rising to the balls of her feet, Vera lifts the point of her right shoe to touch the inside of the opposite knee and balances on one foot. A strong gust of wind, an earthquake, a motherfucking muscle spasm could send her over the edge, but she's worried about perfecting her form.

"Am I holding my chin high enough?" she wonders.

"You're fucking crazy," I say, closing the space between us.

A smile spreads across her face, and she drops her arms to her sides while balancing on a single foot. "Maybe," she says confidently. "But I was made this way, not born."

With the exception of the one person who haunts me in quiet moments, I don't put thought into the people I kill. They're a contract. A deposit in my bank account. A means to an end. A hit is nothing more than a job, and when the job is done, I go home and sleep soundly. Whether it be by natural causes or consequence, people die every day. Not once in the ten years since my first contract have I deliberated the permanence of death. Not once have I considered saving someone instead of letting them die.

Until Vera slips.

Time stops for a single breath, long enough for our eyes to meet.

Long enough to feel the crushing weight of forever.

Long enough to realize I don't want to let her go yet.

Vera screams until her lungs fail, and the cold holds the sound hostage like it did the jasmine and peach. The piercing ring of her fright shatters the stars, and their dying embers come down like rain from the black sky. Moonlight shutters, and the world turns on its axis, falling out of orbit. If the ocean is coming to carry her away on a wave, the son of a bitch is taking too long.

Save her.

Save her, a small voice whispers through the chaos in my head.

Save her.

Fucking save her.

Darting forward puts time in motion, and Vera reaches out with both hands as she falls back. Her wide eyes soften when realization settles in—this is it, this is the end—and it's good I didn't tell her she wouldn't die on the way down. She doesn't need to know that when the falling stops and the dropping starts, she'll meet the ground and feel it.

I collide with the ledge, my boots jamming into the slant where the wall meets the deck. Leaning over the edge, I throw my arms. The concrete barrier cuts into my upper thighs and crushes my kneecaps, but something urges me forward despite the pain. My feet come off the ground just as my fingertips sweep over the front of her shirt, and she falls away from me.

If she goes down, we're going down together. And I'm not dying tonight. Gripping her elbow, I squeeze tight through momentum. Gravity fights back, sinking its fangs into me, tearing muscle from bone. I don't give up or give in, and just before I lose her for good, Vera claws her fingers into my jacket.

"Baby, don't let me go. Hold on. Hold on," I say through gritted teeth.

Vera slams into the ledge, but she holds on to me with the same upper body strength she uses to hold the stripper pole. And I'm glad she's not a fucking ballerina. Scooping her in my arms, I bury my face in her hair and carry her over the threshold onto solid ground.

"Don't put me down," she cries out, circling her arms around my neck. She mauls my shoulders and wraps her legs around me. "Not yet. Don't put me down. Oh my god, don't put me down, Rip."

If she were smaller, I'd cage her behind my rib bones so nothing can threaten her again. Because the universe doesn't give a fuck. I tuck Vera under my chin, belted by my arms, and flattened against my chest as my eyes roam, searching for a lingering threat. All I find are the stars in place, the moon undisturbed, and the planet right on its axis. And the ocean … the ocean serves no one.

I'll break this motherfucking building down brick by brick. Something is going to pay for the trembling girl in my arms.

Her hand slides inside of my jacket, stopping when she feels my gun. When she doesn't cry louder, scream louder, or run, I realize the threat is already trapped in my arms. Gravity didn't take our lives tonight. It stripped me free from rationality and left me, in my barest form, undone.

I should have let her fall.

Wrapping my hands around her upper arms, I squeeze until small bones bend just before breaking and lift her to the tops of her shoes. Violet eyes melt, blackening as her pupils expand, and she gasps. But she doesn't ask what's going on. She knows what this is. That's the problem.

I spin her around, curving my body to fit the contours of hers. With nowhere to go, she doesn't struggle to break free.

"You won't hurt me," she whispers on a shaky breath.

Locking my left arm across her chest, I snake my right

hand over the hollow point between her clavicles. She swallows, tender bones massaging the tips of my fingers as they travel up, up, up, past her racing heartbeat to rest just under each side of her jaw. Tilting her head back to rest against my shoulder, I apply enough pressure so that she understands I'm in control. But it's not enough to render her unconscious. I'm not there yet.

"Wishing out loud?" I ask.

She inhales through her nose, holding on to my wrists as if she's strong enough to pry them away. Racing pulse, wobbly bones, eyes searching for a way out—Vera's appropriately afraid. The fright radiating from her body turns the blood in my veins molten, and I rest my forehead against her temple as my cock hardens against her lower back.

"I will hurt you." I close my eyes and inhale her sweet scent. "I'll steal everything important to you, end your life, and make sure you're never found. I *am* the motherfucking Mafia, Vera. Nothing gets past me, nothing survives me, and you're no exception."

Her mouth parts, but all that comes out is mist from the cold.

"Who sent you to fuck with me?" I pin her between my body and the ledge. She can't see over the edge, but her chest heaves. "I could throw you back over and have the mess cleaned up before sunrise. Who the fuck sent you?"

"No one." She tries to turn her head to look at me, but I tighten my grip.

Playing with my food has never been more appetizing than it is now, and I'm fucking starved. If she's going to play games, I'm going to take more than her life tonight.

I'll take everything.

"Rip," she hums, and I feel the vibration of her plea against the palm of my hand. It has a direct line to my dick, and I groan, running my nose along the shell of her ear. Vera whispers, "No one sent me."

The frigid breeze does nothing to put a damper on the fire raging inside my mind. Engulfed in flames, my hand skims from her throat to her mouth. I part Vera's lips with the tips of my fingers, pressing against her teeth until she opens for me. She bites me at the intrusion, but it only intensifies the hunger pangs.

"You can't beat me." I kiss the side of her face as I sink my fingers farther, cutting myself on her teeth. "I'm going to reach down your fucking throat and squeeze your heart from the inside. Then you'll feel what I'm feeling before I rip it out."

Whining around the intrusion, she squeezes her eyes closed, pushing tears from her eyes. She squirms against my hold, kicking her feet and clawing at my arms. Until she looks up at me with eyes that have lost their color, and I drown in black pools. Vera's grip on my wrists loosens, and she rolls her hips, stroking my aching cock. She gags on my fingers before darting her tongue out and licking between them, urging them farther back. Swirling her tongue around my middle and pointer finger, she sucks them and moans.

She winks.

"Fuck," I hiss, thrusting against her.

Pulling my fingers from her mouth, she licks her lips and smiles. "I've already told you that you don't scare me. I'm not your enemy."

A look.

A pause.

A breath.

Kissing her is like kissing death.

Brutal, ordained, and fucking absolute, the moment Vera's lips touch mine, I recognize the sweet sorrow as the one that lingers inside of me after a kill. The thrill of existing between heaven and hell. It's turning my back on the first commandment and hoping it doesn't catch up to me too soon. It's being a god. A devil. Fate. Vera's kiss is tapping into power I've only ever found on my own before now.

It's a place I can hide.

A place where I can be myself.

Breaking away from the kiss, she drops her head back against my shoulder and pulls in a lungful of air. Rolling my hips, I thrust my cock against her bottom as my hand finds the apex between her thighs and massages.

"Harder," she cries out, riding my hand. Vera reaches back, gripping the collar of my jacket and holding me impossibly closer. Swaying her hips back and forth, she dry fucks the fingers she just sucked on. A teasing smile curves the corner of her mouth, and she whispers between gasps, "Is that it? Give me all you got."

Slipping my free hand under her shirt, I squeeze her breast like I should have her heart. Driven by instinct or desperation, Vera straightens her back and parts her legs, inviting my hand down the front of her jeans. I palm her bare pussy, parting a different pair of lips, before piercing her with my fingers. Filling her to the hilt, I curve my fingers until I find the spot that makes her sing, pressing my thumb against her clit and rubbing.

The grip on my jacket turns gentle as she loosens her hold and glides her hand around the back of my neck. We sway in perfect rhythm, rolling forward, thrusting back, and pushing deeper. When her inner walls clench around me, Vera bites her bottom lip and unravels in the palm of my hand.

She cries out, and this time the moon definitely shutters.

Four

RIP

"How fast can you get to Oakland?" Nicolai Coppola, don of the Coppola crime family, asks.

Holding my cell phone between my face and shoulder, I look down at my watch. It's one a.m., nearly twenty-four hours since I dropped Vera Monroe off in front of a yellow and white Queen Anne on the outer edge of Grand Haven.

"I would have invited you in had you driven me straight home," she'd said, walking backward toward the front door. Her lips were kiss-swollen, and the collar of her shirt was stretched out. *"But I have to be up early."*

After collecting our shipment from the docks earlier this afternoon, we had the six wooden crates labeled as car parts transported to a private warehouse outside town. It's one of the many properties the organization has on rotation away from prying eyes. The same crew that partied at Trinity's last night, pry open the crates, gearing up for a long night of inventory and quality control before these firearms hit the streets.

Stepping out of earshot, I say "Thirty minutes."

"Twenty is better." Nico sighs. The sound of ice turning inside a glass comes through the phone.

I exit the warehouse under a pitch-black sky, flooded only by the yellow-orange security light above the overhead door. "What's up?"

"Marked a Cisneros in our backyard. Oakland is neutral territory, but I don't want those motherfuckers getting too close, if you know what I mean," he explains. His tone is thick with sleep, and he yawns. "Check it out and report back."

"What about the shipment?"

"Damage can handle it, Rip," he says dismissively. "Why are you supervising that shit anyway? And what the fuck are you doing up at this hour? I thought I was going to catch you at home."

Can't get my mind off a girl.

"I'll let you know what I find out," I say, patting my pockets for the keys to my Harley.

"Good." Nico chuckles. "Make it fast and get some shuteye. Our plane leaves at noon. It's only the two of us, after all."

"What about—?"

"Call me after you've dealt with Cisneros, will you?" Nicolai cuts me off. "And make sure those sonsofbitches don't get this close to Grand Haven again."

Reporting my comings and goings was never part of my job description, and it's not a habit I'll start now. My bike announces my departure, the engine roaring across acres of vacant land. The headlights illuminate the unmaintained highway like a spotlight, throwing beams of light against the heavy tree cover on each side of the road.

I pull onto the highway and feed the throttle, sailing

toward the city. My focus should be on the trespassers closing in on our territory, but I'm hard pressed to concentrate on
anything but Vera Monroe.

"Don't be a stranger, Rip," she's said in parting.

Until yesterday, I thought getting the Coppola crown was
the most exciting thing that had happened to me lately. Then
Vera danced into my life under a red light, and I can't remember
the last time someone consumed my thoughts the way she has.

I don't trust her, but she let me hold her over the edge of
a massive drop and finger fuck her with a smile. The feel of
her soft lips, the sweet taste of her skin, and the way she whis-
pered my name once her climax peaked helped convince me.
But she walked away alive because I let her. Vera likes to play
around, and I'm game. For now.

If she has something to hide, I'll figure it out and deal
with it then.

"You know where to find me," Vera said before disappearing inside.

City limits are invisible. Nothing separates Grand Haven
from Oakland but a welcome sign and a four-way intersection.
But the change in scenery is immediate. High-rises shrink into
run-down shopping centers. Upscale seaside restaurants taper
off into liquor stores and street vendors. There are bail bonds-
men and cash-advance shops on every corner. Grand Haven
sleeps soundly at one thirty in the morning, but Oakland
thrives at this time.

Car clubs occupying entire parking lots, street gangs, and
normal civilians working the night shift eye my bike from the
sidewalks and store windows. They won't approach me. They
won't come near me. No sane person rides alone through

Oakland in the middle of the night unless they can back their shit up. There's a difference between real organized crime and what these bastards do. And I don't have to throw up a single sign for them to know where I'm from. Coppolas demand respect.

I'm king.

No one fucks with royalty.

But the streets talk. If a Cisneros is still in the city, they know I'm here and will come to me.

I park my bike in front of Valentino's, a twenty-four-hour pizzeria that serves the best fucking gelato in the area. The savory aroma of baked bread and melted mozzarella makes my mouth water as soon as I step inside the pizza joint. Rushing from the kitchen, the owner, an old-timer with a round stomach and thinning hair, wipes his hands on his apron as he welcomes me back.

"What can I get for you, Rip?" he asks with forced enthusiasm. I respect the effort. "On the house. Anything you want."

"Not necessary, Mikey, but thank you." I throw a hundred-dollar bill on the countertop. "Give me a scoop of lemon gelato, would you?"

"Coming right up, boss." He leaves the money on the counter. Shaking his finger beside his head, he says, "It's my nonna's recipe. God rest her soul."

He retells his family history, just like he does every time I find myself in Valentino's. When he gets to the part of his nonna's immigration from Italy to the United States, Mikey looks up with a proud smile. It pales once I'm distracted by something over my shoulder.

We're not alone.

"Thanks again," I say, taking the cup from him. "Close up for the night. You work too much. It's not good for you."

Shoveling a spoonful of lemon ice into my mouth, I step outside and ignore my company. They came to our house un-invited. They'll wait for me to finish my dessert.

Anthony Cisneros acts as unbothered as I am, standing at the edge of the curb as I lean against the storefront, savor-ing every bite of Nonna Valentino's famous lemon gelato. God bless her for making the trek across the ocean with nothing but two cents to her name. God bless her.

"Have you tried this?" I point to the gelato with the plas-tic spoon. "Best you'll ever have."

Anthony folds his hands at his waist, watching me down the bridge of his nose. "I've had better."

Liar.

Scraping the bottom of my gelato cup for the very last bite, I make a show of finishing it before tossing the trash and wiping the corner of my mouth with my thumb. Then I get down to business, unconcerned with the two men flanking his side. "What are you doing in Oakland?"

Parts of the state are carved out for the Irish and Russian mobs, and other smaller syndicates. But California is predom-inantly controlled by the Italian Mafia. The Coppolas and the Cisneros have California split through the middle, north and south. Our history goes way back, and it's as dark as our peace is thin. This is a big fucking state, and our organizations would love nothing more than the chance to secure more territory—unlevel the playing field. That's why impromptu visits from their underboss can't go unanswered.

"Sightseeing." He shrugs, eyeing me down the bridge of

his nose. He's got about ten years on me, dark eyes, dark hair, with a chip on his shoulder.

One of his bodyguards laughs into his closed fist, and the other, an *American Psycho*–looking motherfucker, looks around at the trash in the gutters and the dirty sidewalks like it offends him.

"Visiting time is over. Time to go," I say.

"This is neutral territory, RIP," Anthony reminds me.

"This *was* neutral territory." I open my jacket to show the gun strapped to my side. Weapons don't scare them, but what I can do with a gun will. "The borders are closed, motherfucker."

He looks over his shoulder to share a look with the psycho. They engage in a silent conversation before Anthony slowly returns his gaze to me. "You have something that belongs to us. We want it back."

"Not possible. Looks like you made the trip here for nothing." I spit at his feet. "Coppolas don't fuck with anything that belongs to a Cisneros."

"You'll return our property or we're coming in for it," he insists.

Stepping into his personal space, I stand an inch taller than him and smile. "I look forward to it."

Pinching the bridge of his nose, Anthony sighs. "Don't you want to know what it is?"

With a swift shake of my head, I say, "No."

Aside from the four of us, there's not another soul in sight. But we have eyes on us. Those too afraid to stand in the light, hide in the shadows, or spy on us through peepholes in doors and behind dusty window treatments. Our families have taken extreme measures to prevent war, but the streets hum with anticipation. Who will strike first? Who can say they were around to witness it happen?

"We heard you took the vow," Anthony says. He puts space between us, trading a defensive expression for one of amusement. "Nico Coppola took his muscle and made him a made man. Since when does the Borgata initiate half Italians? Here's what I think. I think your outfit is weak. Nico is scared, or he's setting you up. Which is it?"

Throwing my head back, I laugh to the moon and stars the same way Vera sang to them the night before. But nothing is funny, and that's why I can't stop laughing. Until I do and the air pressure changes with my mood, low and scorching fucking hot. The night stands still, silent, the only sounds being electricity running up and down lines.

Even Anthony has the mind to look unsure.

"Oh, I'm Italian where it matters." I grab my balls. "Choose your words wisely, Cisneros, because if I don't like what comes out of your mouth next, I'll make sure you choke on this Italian cock before I blow your fucking head off."

Psycho fists his hands, and I welcome him to suck this big dick too.

"This was a courtesy visit," Anthony says. He holds his arm out, calling off the dogs. "Before things get out of hand."

"Here's what I think," I say, turning his words against him. "I think you're full of shit. Leave while you still have legs to walk on because I'm out of patience. And tell your boss the next time a Cisneros shows up uninvited, we're sending them back in pieces. Times have changed, motherfucker. You don't want this smoke. Trust me."

"Things won't end well for you, RIP," Anthony warns,

seemingly unmoved by my threat. Fine with me. I'd like nothing more than to put a bullet between his eyes. "We'll be back to collect what's ours."

Shaking loose the bandanna draped from my pocket, I pull it tight around my mouth and nose and tie the ends at the back of my head. I throw my leg over the Harley, securing my helmet under my chin before lifting the kickstand and turning the engine.

"We went over this," I remind him, letting my back tire spin as I hold the brake. "We don't have your trash."

It's after three in the morning when I get back to the city. I've managed to stay away from her for an entire day, but instead of riding home, I'm drawn to Trinity. There's no way to be sure if Vera's working tonight, but she told me to find her. So, here I am, finding.

I don't have to look for long. Pulling off the highway, I notice the same model SUV that arrived to pick her up last night parked in front of the club. The white-haired driver is nowhere to be seen. In his place is a younger guy wearing an ill-fitted suit, leaned against the front bumper with his arms crossed over his chest. Vera's sitting on the curb with her ankles crossed and her face toward the sky, soaking in the moonlight.

"I almost gave up on you," she says when I arrive, stopping my bike at her feet. Vera's chauffeur stands straight, looking wild-eyed as she hops on. "That poor bastard has been waiting on me for an hour, but I had a feeling you would come."

Unfastening the helmet, I pull it off and pass it back, running my fingers through my hair as I size up the driver. Our eyes meet, and he recoils, scrambling around to the other side of the vehicle. As far as I'm concerned, he's responsible for getting her home. Which means he's responsible for her safety and wellness. I should snap his neck for letting her go without a fight, like a car door could save him from me when I took death on the night before.

But all is forgotten once Vera circles her arms around me and rests her chin on my shoulder.

Then … then there's only jasmine and peach.

Desolation, New York is a mecca for crooks and criminals.

The location was never put up for a vote or selected to be our place to congregate for any particular reason. It just was. The city calls to the immoral.

Once rich in agriculture, Desolation was hit hard by the depression and never recovered. Farms dried up, slaughter-houses and meatpacking plants closed, and the community moved on. What's left now is nothing but abandoned factories, sun-bleached and crumbling after years of neglect. Our rental car, a blacked-out Mercedes Benz, stands out like a sore thumb next to the small stores with chipped paint and broken siding. But the people who've stuck it out and live here know to look the other way. Gangsters are part of the scenery.

"Your first time?" Nico asks, ignoring the scenery. He lifts the collar of his jacket and sinks into the passenger seat before unpocketing a flask and screwing the top off.

"With The Ruin? No," I say, coming to a slow stop at a single-sided traffic light. It squeaks in the winter breeze, sway-ing back and forth on an electric cable. "I accompanied your father a few times. Done jobs for the others when they needed someone outside their outfit."

Nico nods, hissing after a swig. There's a new tattoo on his neck, praying hands and a rosary. Nicolai is covered in religious tattoos, an attempt to wager with God for the life he lives. When his day of judgment comes, what's marked on his body won't matter. But I'm not going to tell him that.

The sun sets as we drive past a faded billboard that reads *Butcher and Son* before parking in front of a deserted factory in what used to be the meatpacking district on the outskirts of town. Neglect has turned the brick building into a nightmare. Entire sections of the roof are missing, the windows are broken out, and the environment has reclaimed what used to be the parking lot and walkways.

"We're not in Grand Haven anymore," I mutter, parking the car.

"Let's get this shit over with." Nico straightens his wool jacket, flipping the switch from reluctant predecessor to the boss he was born to be. He shifts between the two personalities with ease and impeccable timing. With his hand on the door, he turns to me. "Do I have anything in my teeth?" He smiles.

Asshole.

I get out of the car, buttoning my suit jacket upon standing. The designer shoes on my feet shine in the headlights, crushing dry leaves and rocks under the red bottoms like this suit crushes my fucking soul. *Dress for the occasion,* Nico had said. When I took my vow, I promised to represent the Coppola crime family to the fullest. And apparently, I can't do that in Doc Martens.

"You look good," Nico says, standing beside me.

Pulling my tie loose, I look at the dilapidated building and say, "We'd look better if our advisers were here as requested."

Nico tosses a mint into his mouth, masking the scent of liquor on his breath. Breaking it between his teeth, he shrugs and says, "Power stops for no one, and our advisers are two powerful motherfuckers."

"Is that the story we're going with?" I ask with a laugh. We walk toward the factory entrance. "Because I'm sure that will go over well."

The scene in Butcher and Son is an FBI agent's wet dream.

Bosses, underbosses, and their trusted advisers from America's most prolific organized crime operations congregate under one roof like we don't have targets on our backs—from the feds and from each other. The large metal door slams behind us, announcing our arrival with the grace of a car wreck. Conversation carries off the steel walls upon our entrance, low murmurs with some brave laughter. It all stops.

Nico lifts his chin in defiance, and I'm steady at his side, crossing my hands behind my back.

A cold breeze followed us in, but heat fills the room, stifled by tension and mistrust. No guns are allowed at meetings like this, and yet, the looks we receive are loaded. Ranks change from time to time—people get locked up, some die, and others … those deadbeats, cooperate and disappear. But for an outfit to swear in a boss, an underboss, and two advisers in a single night is rare. Now we're standing like products on a display case, and they're sizing us up.

Formal introductions aren't necessary. I don't have to stand from my seat and introduce myself like some chump in a support meeting. They know who I am, or they'll figure it out soon enough. I'm here because it's the fucking rules. I've got a lot of those to follow lately.

"Nicolai." Paulo D'Angelo, a local boss, reaches for Nico's hand and clasps it in both of his. "I was sorry to hear about your father."

Giovanni Guerra, another New York boss, offers his condolences next. Then Leonid Petrov, and his sons, before two more respected dons, Enzo De Rossi and Alexei Koslov, give their sincere apologies.

"Did you get my flowers?" one asks.

"You'll let me know if there's anything you need," another offers.

"He was a good man." Someone sighs. "These things happen to the best of us."

"Any idea who's responsible?" they ask. At this point, their faces and rehearsed sympathies blend together. "When you find out, we have your back. Our families go way back. I don't see why that needs to change now."

It's the who's who of mafiosi, and I'm distracted.

My thoughts are three thousand miles away in Grand Haven.

With a girl who wanted to be a ballerina but mastered the pole instead.

Violet eyes. Deep throat. Death defying.

"Stay," she'd said when I dropped her off at home early this morning. *"Stay with me. You want to."*

I couldn't stay, but that didn't stop her from unscrewing the porch light until it died. She pushed me into the corner under the cover of darkness, and my hip rang the doorbell on impact. Vera lowered to her knees and freed my cock in the same way she'd freed me from control, blatantly and all at once.

She took me in her mouth, and I drove my hands through her hair.

Vera sucked me with tears in her eyes and a twist of her tongue, and when she was done, she stood up and kissed me with my taste on her lips.

"Sure you can't stay?" she asked.

"Can't."

"Can't or won't?"

"Can't."

After she dug around in her purse, Vera held a Sharpie like a sword and wrote her phone number across my palm from thumb to pinky finger. I memorized it, tried to scrub it off in the shower and again in the airport bathroom, but the seven and nine stay trapped in the creases of my hand.

A deep male voice interrupts my reverie, and the room comes back into focus as he says, "I don't like to cause trouble, but between friends, word is the Coppolas let a woman sit at the table during family business."

Nico looks up from his glass of bourbon, a glass I have no recollection of him acquiring, and narrows his eyes. He tilts his head, as if a change in angle will make the audacity of this conversation less invasive.

This is why we're not allowed to carry during these meetings. If I had my guns, Carlo Capone, a big shot from Florida, wouldn't have a fucking head right now.

But I'm resourceful.

Grabbing him by the neck, I crush his windpipe and watch the blood vessels in his eyes burst as his heartbeat quickens with panic before slowing down with demise. I keep a straight face, more at ease with this man's life in my hand than I've been since we arrived at this spectacle. Does he want to measure dicks? Is that what this is? Mine is the biggest.

I'm sure there's a Cisneros around who can attest to it.

A hand clasps my shoulder, patting it twice. "That's enough. He won't be able to talk for a week."

"Too soon," Nico mumbles into his glass, emptying the contents.

Loosening my hold on Capone's throat, I'm amused to see the color drain from his face as he wheezes for a lungful of air he can't capture. His men realize there's been a disturbance and hurry over, pushing up their sleeves for a fight. Nicolai sets his glass down and sighs, rolling his head from side to side. Before we can knuckle up, Astore De Marco, the man behind the hand on my shoulder and boss out of Philly, steps between the commotion. It's enough to keep the Capone crew back. No one crosses Astore and lives. Not on the streets of Philadelphia, not in Desolation, and not in The Ruin, where we're supposed to be on even ground.

"Let the man go, Rip," he says in a bored tone, dismissing Carlo's men with a curt nod.

I squeeze harder before releasing him, because I don't take orders from anyone outside my family, but also because he's right.

We are not allowed to kill each other without a vote.

Rules are rules.

At least, that's how it's supposed to be.

In a move more humiliating than nearly being choked to death in an abandoned warehouse chocked full of colleagues,

Capone stumbles back, unsteady on his feet. He coughs and paws at his throat, tripping over his shoelaces and colliding with an old metal staircase.

He would have been better off dead. At least there's honor in that.

"Carlo, don't talk about what goes on at another man's table," Astore calls out as he tries to keep a straight face. "This is all water under the bridge. Do you understand me?"

Eyes streaked with red shift between Nico, De Marco and me. Carlo opens his mouth to speak, but he can't get a word past the splinters in his throat.

"Water under the bridge," Astore repeats with a ring of finality.

Coppolas aren't chumps, and now we've proven ourselves in the only possible way tonight. A level of tension makes a break for it with Carlo, the doors slamming closed after his exit. I have the mind to chase him down and finish what I started once I notice the numbers seven and nine came clean on his neck. He doesn't deserve Vera in any capacity, not even the ink she stained on me.

"It's good to see you, Rip. You've always kept things interesting." De Marco holds his hand out, and I shake it. Firm and decisive.

"Vita della festa." *Life of the party.* Nicolai chuckles, clapping my back. "He's been this personable since we were kids, believe it or not."

"Pleased to hear you took the vow. You're one of us now," Astore says. "The transition from gunman to administration isn't easy, but you'll adapt. Give it time."

"I'm adapting just fine," I grumble, meeting his stare.

Holding his hands up in surrender, Astore lifts his eyebrows. "All I meant is your only form of communication won't always be murder. Once you get a hang of the politics, choking someone to death will be plan B."

Nico and De Marco share a laugh, holding each other by the back of their necks as they embrace like old, familiar friends. That's the difference between Nico and me. He was born into this life—a prince who inherited the kingdom. By blood. By title. By principle.

Me? I'm just the life of the party.

The Mafia is nothing without ritual. When I got an invitation to the initiation ceremony a few weeks ago, I assumed it was because Nicolai wanted me to handle whoever challenged his reign. He surprised me by lifting his glass in my honor. He said there had been a vote. The job was mine. I'd earned it. Everyone clapped.

But did I earn it? Had my work amounted to more than the effort Damage had accomplished for the organization? He was in the thick of it. Dressing in suits and networking is a job tailored for those who can hold a conversation and refrain from strangling an untouchable, like Frank. But Frank isn't an underboss. I am.

"No one in this room would be sorry if Carlo fell victim in a horrible accident, if you know what I mean," Astore says sometime later. He and Nico polish off a bottle of whiskey, ties loose and eyes heavy. He circles his finger around the room, gesturing to those left in attendance. "It may not feel like it, but none of us can do this alone. We need each other. And the Coppola's need friends now more than ever."

"What the fuck does that mean?" Nico asks.

Holding his hand above his head to indicate something of great height, Astore says, "California is at the top of the food chain. Nothing major happens unless we have your say-so. Hush is expanding. Your choice in consiglieres was interesting. It makes me wonder what involvement you have with Ri—"

"What's your point?" I ask.

"Have you seen a Cisneros tonight? Anyone at all?"

Scratching the back of his neck, Nico shakes his head and asks, "Do you think they'll make a move on our territory. That would mean a war."

"You have our attention, Nico." Again, he nods toward the heads of the other families. "Everyone is watching you. Waiting to see what kind of leader you are. California is a gold mine. You can't afford to show weakness, and Cisneros is making the rounds, dropping hints that the Coppolas aren't who they used to be."

"I have nothing to prove to those fucking snakes." Nico pushes his glass away.

"We have everything to prove, Nico," I say.

Fuck the suit and networking. Give me adversity. Give me a challenge. Put a face to an opponent and watch me break it in half. This is what I'm good at.

I can end a war before it starts.

Astore points to me, wagging his finger. "He's not lying. Your administration is young—really fucking young. You've got a half Italian underboss, a woman calling shots, and two of your members are practically movie stars. My girl was flipping through a magazine the other day, and guess who was on the cover? Your fucking advisers. Craziest shit I've ever seen. But goddamn, they're pretty."

Exhaling from my nose, I pull the tie free from around my neck. "If they move in on us, it'll be the last thing they do. It'll be the last thing any of you do."

Nodding, De Marco turns to Nico and says, "Our families have history. We have your back. A lot of honorable men in this room have your back." He turns to me and smiles. "Don't kill your friends. You never know when you might need them."

Five

Don't kill your friends.

Vera locks her front door and comes bouncing down the steps in lace socks and a pair of Docs just like mine. Her hair is curled today, poured over her shoulders like an oil spill reflecting the sun off its dark surface. I breathe out, smooth between my lips, admiring how her curves fill out the black and green plaid schoolgirl skirt she's in. I've seen her in less, but how her belly barely peeks out from under her shirt makes me ache.

The last thing I want to do right now is kill anyone.

Not when she's this beautiful, and I'm this caught up.

"For me? Or is that for all the girls you take for a ride?" she asks as she approaches.

Leaning against my bike, I stand straight with the helmet I picked up for her earlier today. "No one rides my bike but me."

Knowing eyes meet mine. "And me."

"And you," I say, setting the helmet on her head. A smile curves the corner of my mouth. "If I'm going to stop killing my friends, I may as well start easy."

Vera lifts to the tips of her boots, still a head shorter than me, and slides her arm over my shoulder. Her fingertips dance at the nape of my neck, and she licks her lips, wetting them before they spread into a smile. The helmet falls back on her head as my hand slides up her thigh, sneaking under her skirt.

"Hadn't heard from you in a few days. I'm glad you called," she whispers, bringing my face closer to hers. "Where are you taking me?"

Staring at her full lips, I ask, "Any early morning appointments tomorrow?"

"What day is it today?"

I have to think about it—truly think about it, paddling through the haze she has me under. Instinct. Reason. Self-awareness. All gone. Her sweet scent mutes the salty perfume of the ocean in the air, decaying leaves on the ground, and my bike's cooling motor, turning the dial all the way down while turning me all the way up. I focus on the sound of the breath coming in and out of Vera's lungs, remembering the way she screamed at the stars and moon when she came on my hand less than a week ago. And how she tasted when I licked it from my fingers.

She's distracting.

Dangerous.

She's a gun pointed at the back of my head, and I didn't see it coming.

"Nope," she says. Her lips wait a breath away from mine. "My schedule is clear on Sundays. I'm all yours."

Slipping beneath the fabric of her thong, I palm her bare ass and dig my fingers in. "You shouldn't say those things to me, Vera."

She flicks her tongue out to lick from my chin to my bottom lip. "But I like the way your eyes change when I do."

This isn't the first time she's mentioned the way my eyes change color. The first was when I stalked her on the roof of Ridge & Sons. My intentions are different now, more savage than lethal. But it's a sobering reminder that I don't trust her. I'll kill her when I have to. Because women like her don't appear out of nowhere, and men like me should know better.

"Let's ride." I nod toward the bike. "Those underwear are going to give everyone a show."

Vera laughs. "That's kind of my thing."

Taking her anywhere inside Grand Haven is out of the question. In a city this small, I'd run into one of my guys and never live it down. I can endure a little ball busting from those who work beneath me. It's the ones I work beside who concern me. The ones I share a table with, make decisions with. Vera weakens my resolve, but Nico, Frank, and the others don't need to know that. She's none of their business.

We ride north.

Out of Grand Haven, past San Francisco, evading the setting sun down a long stretch of highway that runs parallel with the coast. Ocean spray dampens our clothes, the salty air burns our eyes, but the open road is freeing. For miles and miles, I'm not a killer, and she doesn't dance for money. We exist with the sky, the redwoods, and the draining daylight.

As the traffic thins and the highway narrows from four lanes to two, Vera's grip around my middle lessens, and she lifts her face from between my shoulders. Looking back and forth between the road and the side mirror, I catch glimpses of her sunning her face, eyes closed with the wind moving through her hair.

I set the cruise control and keep one hand on the bars, hooking the other behind her knee.

"Can we keep going?" she asks, sliding her hands from my sides to my shoulders. "Never go back?"

She can't see me smile beneath the bandanna tied around my head, and I don't recognize the feeling of it on my face. My chest fills with warmth, and it quickly spreads down to my stomach and through my limbs. Indifference thaws, shedding sheets of ice from around my heart like melting glaciers, and I choke on my heartbeat.

Fuck.

"Don't crash, okay? I want to try something." Before I can stop her, Vera digs her heels in and stands up with a death grip on my shirt.

"Vera," I groan, downshifting. A ripple of panic moves through me like the night she almost fell from the roof.

"No, don't slow down," she begs.

This girl will be the end of me.

Resetting the cruise control, I zero in on the road, the sky, and cars coming and going down the highway, hyper focused on spotting potholes, distracted drivers, rogue motherfucking birds and asteroids—anything that threatens her safety. She releases her hold on my right shoulder, stretching her fingers toward the darkening sky, laughing with joy as she cuts through the wind.

It catches beneath her skirt, raising it above her waist as a blue sedan approaches from behind. The moment the driver realizes Vera's whole ass is exposed, they slam on the brakes before thinking twice and picking up speed to pass. The man behind the wheel laughs, paling when the woman in the passenger seat swats him with the back of her hand. The kid in the back looks in love, pressing his face against the window to catch Vera shaking her bottom suggestively.

The woman reaches back and smacks him, too.

Once they drive off, Vera leans down and whispers, "How much farther?"

"Twenty minutes."

"I can't wait that long," she says.

With the grace of a ballerina and the talent of a pole dancer, Vera hitches her leg around my front and slides on to my lap. The bike swerves into oncoming traffic as she settles against me, rolling her hips and pressing our chests together. I correct the front wheel, circling my arm around her waist to keep her steady.

"You're fucking insane," I say, torn between keeping my eyes on the road or on her.

She pulls the bandanna down my face, violet eyes shifting back and forth between mine and my mouth. And then we're kissing. Dirty, wet, worshiping, Vera cradles my chin in her firm hand, and I fist the back of her shirt with enough force, threads break. Our lips move together, tongues touching, forgetting to breathe, forgetting we're speeding down the fucking highway on a motorcycle.

"I'm going to dump the bike if we don't stop," I say, tasting spearmint on her breath.

Smiling against my kiss, Vera says, "It'll be a good death."

We're not dying tonight. Not when living feels this good.

She drags her lips across my jaw and down my neck, slow

and hot, grazing her teeth over my pulse point, lighting me up. The sway of her hips starts off slowly, swinging up and back, around and around as her tongue and lips play from my throat to my ear.

"Pull over," she whispers, upping her pace, digging in deep. Vera touches my lips with hers, reaching between us to unfasten my belt. My cock is hard, throbbing against the inseam of my jeans.

Vera's hands are unsteady, and she gives up on the belt, instead slipping needy palms under the hem of my shirt. Her smooth touch slides up my sides before dragging sharp fingernails down to my waist, drawing a moan from me. I lift her higher onto my lap, hitching her over my throbbing erection. "I can fuck you on the bike. Right now. Just like this," I say, sucking her bottom lip into my mouth possessively.

Her nails stake claim in my skin. "I want to live long enough to do it more than once. To do it fast and hard."

With her open thighs on each side of me, I keep one hand on the bars and inch the other from her knee to her hip. Trembling under my touch, she drops her head back and gasps as I slip under her panties, parting her sex open with the pad of my thumb. I stroke the length of her pussy, circling her clit with slick arousal.

"Damn," I rasp. My mouth fills with saliva, craving the taste of her pleasure.

Another car draws near, filled with a group of guys dressed in pastel polo shirts and golf caps. They roll their windows down and cheer as they pass, one yelling, "Show us your tits!"

If I wasn't knuckle deep in Vera's cunt, I'd shoot their tires out just to watch the car flip and erupt in fire. And I wouldn't slow down or piss on them to save their sorry lives. Vera isn't bothered by their rudeness, laughing with strands of hair stuck to her lips, all too willing to be fucked on a Harley Davidson going fifty miles an hour down the highway. When forty-five minutes ago, she had her knees tucked against the bike and her face hidden in my shoulder, terrified as I split lanes to get through traffic.

Afraid one moment. Fearless the next.

She doesn't overcompensate like a normal girl, a try-hard looking for a way to relate. And she's not derelict like a princi-pessa, who doesn't need to relate to a goddamned thing.

The problem is Vera is both.

She's a secret keeper.

The compulsive part of my personality wants to slit her fucking throat. Fuck a clean shot. Let's make this up close and personal—messy, sticky, passionate.

The other side of me, the detached part, likes the shape of her lips when she whispers, "Rip, please." It wants to attach— messy, sticky, passionate.

Kill and fuck.

Or fuck and then kill.

We're absolutely fucking.

But why haven't I killed her?

Why didn't I let her die?

Any moment spent with me is dangerous, but when fate made its move, I risked my neck to save her life.

She's a siren, and I'm on alert. But it's more than this hard cock and her sweet pussy. I can fuck anyone. The problem is violet eyes have burned a hole in my head, and when I think about hurting her instead of finding out what she's hiding, it feels like a stabbing.

And yeah, it's the shape of my name on her mouth.

"Please, Rip." She holds my hand to her center, using her fingers to guide my fingers through her heat. "You're driving me crazy."

After a curve in the highway, I steer the bike off the road onto the unpaved shoulder. It's bumpy driving over dips in the gravel and fallen foliage, and Vera gasps, wrapping her arms around my neck. We come to a skidding halt alongside a thick cover of trees swaying in the cool ocean breeze. A cloud of dust blooms around us, carried away as a semitruck speeds by.

Vera exhales, warm against my neck where she's hidden her face. I turn the bike off and lower the kickstand, not thinking twice about leaving it on the side of the road as I carry Vera past the tree line. Nervous breaths quickly turn back into burning kisses as the sounds of the highway disappear behind us.

Giant redwoods extend their reach toward the sky, their branches weaving together like veins to block out the sun. I lower Vera onto her back beside one and kneel between her thighs, my knees sinking into the soft dirt. With hooded eyes, she watches me remove my shirt, blinking slowly as she takes in the ink across my chest that continues down my arms to my hands.

Her nipples harden, pebbling through her thin top, when I unbuckle my belt like she couldn't.

"Would you believe me if I told you this isn't why I asked you out?" I lower my zipper, leaving my jeans loose as I reach under Vera's skirt for her underwear.

She raises her hips, letting me pull black lace down her plush thighs. "Not even a little bit."

"Good girl," I say, wrapping her thong around my hand.

We share a smile. There's not a lot we know about each other, but one thing has been clear since the moment we met: the sex will be hot as fuck.

She lifts her skirt to expose the heat between her legs, delicate, supple, and so motherfucking wet and ready, spreading herself wide for me. I groan with need and reach for my cock, jerking myself with lace.

"Don't ever trust me, Vera." I lean down to kiss the inside of her knee, my chest rumbling as she trembles beneath me. "You're going to get hurt in the end."

"Give me what you got," she says breathlessly, palming her tits as my mouth travels lower, and lower, and lower. "I can handle it."

Lying on my stomach between Vera's legs, I thrust into my fist one more time before hooking both arms around her thighs. I pull her close, holding her hips down with nowhere to go. Not that she's in any hurry to escape.

"You're beautiful, baby," I whisper, a breath away from her sex.

"Not a lie," she says.

"No," I say. "Not a lie."

I lick the entire length of Vera, savoring every inch of her on my tongue. She smells soft and tastes like a rush, and I press in for more, opening my mouth wider, eating everything she's serving. I suck her clit and watch her come undone, thrusting my hips to ease the ache that spreads deep into my stomach.

Her chest rises on a gasp and falls with a moan, and she releases her hold on my hair to dig lines in the damp soil.

"Oh, my god," she rasps, trapping my head between her thighs. "Oh, fuck, Rip. Fuck."

As wild as the creatures that live among the sequoias, Vera's moans ricochet against the ancient trees. Everything quiets, like the forest itself seeks to soak in her breathy desire. I sink into her opening, dragging her body forward to fuck my tongue. Her boots dig grooves into the ground at my sides, and she paws at my arms with her dirty fingers.

"I've never tasted anything as good as you," I say, stamping slow kisses on the inside of her trembling thighs. "There's only one thing that would be better than you coming in my mouth."

"What's that?" she asks as I climb up her body, brushing my nose along the column of her neck.

Against the shell of her ear, I whisper, "Feeling you come around my cock."

In one swift motion, she shoves her palms into my chest and sits up, pushing me onto my calves. *This is it,* I think to myself. The girl has finally smartened the fuck up and is ready to run for her life. I'm equal parts relieved and murderous, hoping she can outrun me as my body readies for a chase.

Reaching for her boots, Vera unties the one on the left. I grip her wrist and say, "Leave them on."

She has a better chance at outrunning me with them on.

Jerking her arm free, Vera searches my expression and rolls her eyes. She loosens her boots, the brand-new leather stiff, and reaches inside to reveal a gold foil square held between her middle and pointer fingers. "How many times do I need to say it? You don't scare me. But unplanned pregnancies do."

"Jesus," I say under my breath, shaking my head. "Where the fuck did you come from?"

Vera holds the condom between her lips and unbuttons my jeans with both hands, keeping eye contact until she releases my dick. The gold packet falls from her mouth, and her eyes fall to my cock. She draws her bottom lip between her teeth as she takes in my length, impossibly hard with a bead of cum at the tip. The veins are engorged and straining for release, the feeling more intense under her stare.

"I know what you mean, Rip." A smirk curves her lips. "Because I've had you come in my mouth before, and it's pretty fucking amazing."

This is her last chance. If she's going to come to her senses and see me for who I really am, this is the time. Once I've had her. Once I'm inside of her. Once I've been inside of her, there's no going back. I'll never let her walk away.

I should say something.

Warn her. Try harder to make her realize the fire she's playing with is zero percent contained.

But why would I do that?

I'm the bad guy.

Ripping the condom open with her teeth, Vera rolls it down my shaft and leans back on her elbows. She invites me in, tilting her head back to open her throat to my mouth, and spreading her knees to open her softness to my hardness.

"You're fucked now." I hitch her leg in the bend of my elbow and fall on top of her. The head of my cock slips through her sex, dropping into place at her entrance.

Sucking in a sharp breath at the slight intrusion, Vera rolls her hips to take me deeper and says, "I look forward to it."

The sun vanishes behind the horizon, dragging away with it the last moments of daylight. The sleepy forest, quieted by Vera's moans, is shaken wide awake with her screams. The moon recognizes the sounds and glows sharp enough to pour beams of white light through the ceiling of branches, tiny spotlights on her pleasure.

Tears spill from the corners of her eyes, down her temples, into her hair. I lick them away one by one, holding the salty drop of moisture on the tip of my tongue before swallowing. I don't fit, and as much as my body yearns to split her in half, we move slow. I roll my hips in painful rotations, gliding in little by little at an agonizing pace. I let her leg down and slide my forearm under her bottom, finding space inside of her to take up. She's stretched tight around me, hot and soaking wet. Breakable.

"Have you done this before?" I ask playfully, resting my forehead on hers.

Holding on to my hips, Vera urges me forward. "All the fucking time."

Her words hit swift and hard, like a nuclear fucking bomb. But I'm not bothered by her sexual history. I accept it like a challenge, keyed up by the opportunity to fuck her so hard and so thoroughly she forgets about anyone but me. I start by carving out my fit, thrusting my hips past the resistance, driving her up from the floor.

"Are you sure you want to provoke me?" I ask, pulling back and slamming into her again.

She cries out, voice thick with tears as I unleash on her body. Vera arches her back, not to get away from me, but to lean in closer—to leave less space between us. Hooking her ankles under my thighs, she pushes through the pain, biting her lip, and drives me forward, faster. We fit like a bullet fits in the chamber of a gun, and she cries out like the barrel is pointed at her head. She gets off on it. Vera likes the pain.

There're tears in her eyes and sobs on her lips, but she moves her hips to meet mine stroke for stroke until the pain turns into indulgence.

"So good," she says, tone thick with passion. "This is so fucking good."

When we come, my lips firm on the side of her throat, and her nails piercing my skin, shattering the night with the collision of our bodies, I don't know if I wiped out her memory of anyone else or if she took out mine. Because as I lie on top of her, my heart beating like a fucking drumline, there's absolutely nothing beyond this. Nothing before. Nothing after.

Everything's violet.

Once I catch my breath, I push away from the ground and get on my feet, discarding the condom to be picked up before we leave. Vera holds her hands to her reddened face, watching me as I tuck myself away and run a hand through my hair.

"What the fuck was that?" I ask, unable to even put a name to it. Unable to pinpoint what the heavy sensation inside my chest means.

Out of breath and boneless under streaks of moonlight, she says, "I know, right?"

Mud is caked in the soles of her booths, stuck between her fingers, and smeared along her skin. She sits up with leaves tangled in her matted hair, watching me like a feral animal ready to pounce. Scrambling to her knees, her teeth are like fangs when she smiles, and I take a step back.

"We should probably—"

She's up before I finish my sentence, jumping into my arms with enough force to knock me back. My ass lands on the cool ground, and Vera tumbles on top of me to straddle my waist. She hikes up her skirt and then reaches into her other boot for a second condom. Breaking it open, she spits out the shredded corner and says, "We're not done yet. It's been so long, and we have nowhere to be but here. It's just us, Rip. Just us."

Six

RIP

The plan was to ride the coastline and catch a nice dinner somewhere with a view.

Not my thing, but she's a lady.

What happens instead is we fuck in the woods until she runs out of condoms. Then we stumble to the bike, caked in dirt with twigs in places they shouldn't be, turned all the way out. On the way back to Grand Haven, we come upon a dive bar with no windows and a flickering sign out front promoting cheap drinks and a steak dinner.

We sit in the back and order two sodas and two New York strips. Vera asks for hers bloody, but I'm not a fucking barbarian, and order my steak medium.

"Best date ever," she says, pulling a dry leaf from her hair.

A neon bar light above our table blinks on and off, buzzing with static electricity. Behind us, a wall of automated dartboards promises that every player is a winner. And across the bar, a mechanical bull with one horn and a cracked saddle spins in slow circles. The wood floors are sticky, a man at the bar is smoking a cigar, and I'm pretty sure the steaks will be inedible. But Vera seems happy.

"This isn't what I had in mind," I admit. Our server drops off our drinks and rushes off to check on our meals.

Swiping a basket of nuts from the table beside ours, her boots leave clumps of drying mud on the dirty floor. She smells like tree bark, damp moss, and good sex, smirking with swollen lips and rosy skin. "I thought it was perfect," she says softly, peeking under her long lashes. "There's nothing I would have changed."

Fascinated by her audacity to be shy after the way we spent the last couple of hours, I put an end to her worries. "You are perfect, Vera. That's not what I meant." Thinking back to the confusion I felt after our first time in the forest, words evade me. I don't have the experience to put a name to the tight feeling in the pit of my stomach, the blast of heat in my palms, or the yearning to reach across the table to hold her hand. "But you might not feel the same when our dinner is served. I should have done more."

We leave a lot left unsaid. What's one more thing? I'd hoped fucking her would put an end to this infatuation, but it's only made it worse. And what am I supposed to do about it? Spill my guts? Tell her how I feel? How do I manage that when I don't know what this feeling is? It changes minute by minute. Fuck and kill.

And now that the fucking part is over…

"How long have you been in Grand Haven?" I ask, swallowing burning coals. "My guys tell me you're new at the club."

Spinning the straw in her cup, Vera pauses at the sudden change in conversation and considers me before pushing the entire cup away. Conflict is easy. I have names for the tension in my jaw and itch in my trigger finger. Mistrust. Frustration. Hazardous.

"Fine. I'll bite," she says, crossing her arms over her chest. "But this isn't a one-sided interrogation. Because from what I can see, there's only two types of people who come into Trinity. Gangsters and the filthy rich. And apparently, you're not who they say you are."

"I'm not a hit man." *Not anymore*, I think to myself.

She nods skeptically, slow and exaggerated. "I didn't peg you as the greedy good ol' boy type. The men in this city are sickening, and it's not their money that offends me. At least the gangsters are honest about what they want."

Scrubbing the palms of my hands down my face, I laugh to myself. How did this get turned around on me?

"A year ago, I went looking for a new start and ended up in Grand Haven," she concedes. "The rest doesn't matter because I'm exactly where I need to be right now. Stop trying to fuck this up, Rip."

"What aren't you telling me?" I ask, even as my heart pounds.

Exhaling heavily, Vera's shoulders drop like this conversation is beating her down. "Today has been one of the best days of my life. Can that be enough?"

"That would be enough for anyone else. I'm not anyone else."

"Why does it matter?"

"Because you're right about the type of people in Grand Haven."

"And which one are you?" she asks.

"I'm the kind of person who will do anything to protect my family." *My oath.* Until two weeks ago, that was the solid truth. Now she's the only exception, and the lie burns my tongue.

We let the sounds of the bar fill in the space between us, a distraction from the realities we're circling around. The cigar smoker at the bar laughs hard enough to puncture a lung, and he beats on his chest to reverse decades of nicotine abuse. At the serving station, our waitress refills the salt shakers while waiting on our steaks and drops the box, groaning, "I hate my job." Another customer walks through the door, letting in a cool rush of air to wash away the stale odor of mold and greasy food. There's a woman at the jukebox, shaking a handful of quarters, flipping back and forth between the same two songs.

I have a mark on every soul in the building, eavesdropping on their conversations and zeroing in on their mannerisms to weed out any threats. But it fades to black when Vera's expression softens and she smiles, turning the full force of her purple stare on me. She reaches across the table and takes my hand, lacing our fingers together beside the basket of peanuts.

"My life is complicated. I dance at the club, fulfill my appointments, and do what I have to do to stay afloat. That doesn't leave a lot of room for socializing. We're having fun together. For the first time in my life, I feel like I have a friend."

"Is that what you're calling this?" I ask, my tone thick with amusement. "A friendship?"

"Not sure. Do friends fuck in the woods like wild beasts?" She grins, squeezing my hand. "If so, I think I need to make a lot more friends. You're busy a lot."

Our waitress, still flustered from the salt, arrives with

our plates, and asks, "Which one of you ordered the steak well done?"

Instead of sending them back, Vera and I carve into our slabs of meat with dull knives and chew until our jaws ache. There's not enough steak sauce in the state of California to mask the taste of charcoal I get with every dry bite.

"This isn't going to work." Eating our meal is hard labor. She drops her fork and knife and picks up the steak with her bare hands, biting right into it.

Untamed seems to be our theme.

The dinner special came with a side of vegetables, and I sample the broccoli, spitting it out when I meet the icy center. "Jesus Christ, this is terrible. I'm a horrible fucking date."

Vera nods in agreement, gnawing on her steak when my phone vibrates in my pocket. Wiping my hands on a paper napkin, it comes apart and sticks to my fingers instead.

"Just use your jeans," Vera says, laughing as I try to shake torn pieces of tissue-like paper from my hands.

"That's rude," I say, pushing my chair back.

"Oh, that's where you draw the line? Table manners?" She licks steak sauce from the corner of her mouth.

The last few hours with Vera have been an escape from the day-to-day grind. Stepping outside feels like backtracking, but reality is as cold and dark as the winter night. "Yeah," I say, answering my phone.

"We've been summoned," Nico says through the receiver, ending his sentence with a drunken laugh. "Need me to pick you up on my way to the building?"

"What time?" I ask, checking the time. It's nine thirty p.m.

"Midnight."

The Mafia doesn't give a fuck if I'm on a date. The operation comes first. No days off. No paid sick time. No excuses. When it calls, I come running. "I thought we planned this for tomorrow night. What's up?"

"Plans changed, Rip," he says. I listen to him unscrew a bottle cap and pour himself a drink. "Do you need me to come by and get you or not?"

Pinching the bridge of my nose, I ask, "Do I need to come by and get *you*?"

He chuckles. "Don't be late."

Exhaling a large breath, I wonder if the sudden change in plans has anything to do with me. Vera and I weren't exactly hiding today. Maybe we were spotted by a rat, and this could be my comeuppance. The rule is simple: don't cross Lydia Montgomery. Just because Vera dances in Lydia's slut mill doesn't mean she owns her. No money was exchanged. No rules broken. Not as far as I'm concerned.

What's the worst that can happen? A slap on the wrist? A stern talking-to?

I'm the motherfucking underboss of the Coppola crime family. I'm untouchable.

Our table is empty when I return. Every table is empty. Garth Brooks's "Friends in Low Places" plays from the jukebox, and I follow the crowd across the bar. The entire place is singing, loudest on the hook before losing the lyrics. The bartender dishes out shots, our waitress fulfills beer orders, even the black lung has left his seat to join the fun. And in the center of it all, riding the one-horned mechanical bull is my date.

As if they can sense my wickedness, the crowd parts as I approach. Careful not to touch.

Vera rides the bull like she rode me in the forest, gentle and methodical, with a look of pure determination on her face. Gripping the machine between her thighs, she digs her heels in and rides the wave, leaning forward and then back with the bull. It spins in complete circles, bucking up and down, but Vera's steady with dirty knees and a relaxed smile. No one can take their eyes off of her, but when she looks up, it's for me.

Friends in low places. She's funny.

"That's right, sweetheart," the cigar smoker mutters lower under his breath, chewing on the end of his fake Cuban. "Ride that shit."

He makes the mistake of looking at me for confirmation, like I'd join in on his perversion. This man with one foot in the grave is lucky I don't put the cigar out in his eyes. He doesn't deserve to look at someone as beautiful as Vera.

"Say something?" I ask him. He doesn't pose a real threat, but my body gears up for a fight. Tense jaw. Tight muscles. Trigger finger willing and ready.

Shaking his head, the man shuffles away, careful to check over his shoulder as he goes to make sure I'm not on his heels.

Leaning against the rail, I watch Vera go around and around a few more times with a smirk on my lips. The bull operator tries to buck her off, and I consider breaking his fucking neck for doing it, but my girl hangs tight. When the song ends, she jumps off and stomps across the padded platform in her boots.

"Is our date over?" she asks, fanning her face with her hands.

"My hands are tied." I move a strand of hair from across her lips.

"Sounds hot." She winks.

Sliding my arm over her shoulders, I tuck her against my body and kiss the top of her head. Vera slips her hand into my back pocket, reaching up with the other to lace our fingers together. After that, a moment doesn't pass when we're not touching. I lift her onto the bike, and she holds on to my sides as I fasten her helmet. On the ride back, she doesn't climb onto my lap again but presses herself close, wrapping her arms tightly around my stomach.

I spend every spare second I have kissing her on the front porch of the yellow Queen Anne.

"Come inside," she whispers against my mouth. "Don't go. Don't go."

"Baby, I have to."

She runs after me when I try, after another kiss, another touch, another chance to get me to stay. I'm often avoided and never the center of anyone's attention, so when Vera pulls me toward the door and says, "I don't want you to go." I don't trust her, but I believe her. And I don't hate being wanted.

Riding away is impossible, but I took an oath. Family first. Family first always. I leave her with a promise to call, but maybe I'll come back after the meeting. The night doesn't have to be over yet, just on hold. An intermission. The roof, the bike, fucking on the forest floor was nice, but to have her in a bed, warm and open…

I swing by my place to shower, my cock lengthening as snapshots of our evening plays on repeat behind closed eyelids. Hot water rains down on my face, streaming over my shoulders and down my back. I grip the base of my dick, stroking myself and wishing it was her. But I can't go to this meeting like this. Focus. I need to fucking focus.

Blood money has afforded me a luxurious life. I stand atop a mountain of dead bodies, but I do it in a condo with a view, expensive clothes in my closet, and a black-on-black Mercedes Maybach parked next to my Harley. The twenty-four-hour valet attendant in my building brings my car around, and I tip well in exchange for his discretion. My comings and goings are private.

"Have a good night, Mr. Alessi." He holds the door open for me.

Unbuttoning my suit jacket, I climb in behind the wheel and exit the circular driveway as a second attendant pulls around in a white Lamborghini Huracan. Adjusting the rearview mirror, I roll down the windows to let in the salty breeze and turn up the music, heading downtown to Ridge & Sons.

The Huracan zooms past me on the highway.

"Asshole," I mutter, pressing on the gas to catch up.

Wilder and Talent Ridge own Grand Haven.

They're America's golden boys.

And they're in the Mafia.

When their father passed away, they inherited Ridge & Sons, a fast-growing litigation law firm, its worldwide prestige, and his association with the outfit. They took their oaths on the same night as me, turning their laundering business agreement with the Coppolas into a lifelong commitment as our consiglieres.

Fitting, considering they've bossed everyone around since we were ten years old.

I turn into the Ridge & Son's parking garage, taking the spot next to Talent's Huracan, Wilder's Mercedes, and a black town car. We share looks of acknowledgment, but Wilder, the older of the two brothers, heads directly to the elevators alone, and Talent helps Lydia out of the passenger seat. He keeps his palm on her lower back, using himself as a barrier between us.

"Where's Nico?" he asks as I exit the car, rebuttoning my jacket.

Before I can ask him the same thing, a black SUV pulls into the garage. I recognize the white-haired chauffeur as the man who arrived to drive Vera home the night we met at the club. He comes to a slow stop, tipping his hat in recognition from behind the wheel as Nico materializes from the back seat.

"This meeting couldn't be an email?" He laughs dryly at his own joke.

Nicolai is the only one who laughs.

We take the service elevator to the top floor, coming one level short of the roof. My thoughts immediately draw back to Vera, and the way she danced on the ledge beneath a blanket of stars. Right before she fell, and everything changed.

"Rip," Nico calls me. He points toward the Ridge & Sons waiting room over his shoulder while I linger in the elevator cab. "You coming or what?"

Was I so distracted I missed the stop?

Clearing my throat, I continue forward like I own the place. When the truth is, until a couple of weeks ago, I'd never stepped foot in this building. My job was to keep watch out-side and eliminate anyone who got too close. Now as Nico's second, my place is at the table.

The table is inside Wilder and Talent's boardroom, where I assume they negotiate legitimate billion-dollar deals during business hours. At midnight once a month, it's used to discuss how much of the Coppola's money they've cleaned with those big-dollar deals. The mob has officially entered the corporate market, and from what I've heard, we're shaking it up.

"Nico, you're at the head of the table," Wilder says, drop-ping a stack of folders "We usually have everything ready, but—"

"Get held up at another photo shoot?" I ask sarcastically, taking the seat at Nico's right. "Who was it for this time? Teen Vogue?"

"Teen Vogue?" Wilder shoots back. "You've acted like a little girl since we were kids, Rip. I'm not surprised you're fa-miliar with Teen Vogue. Do you fill out the quizzes in the back? *Does your favorite pizza topping match your personality?*"

Nico snorts. "He's not an Italian sausage."

"I'm half Italian, motherfucker," I correct him with a side-eye.

"You're Canadian bacon, white boy." He slaps his palm on the table, laughing at his own jokes again.

"No, he's that shit everyone is afraid to eat." Wilder rubs his palms together in thought, his wedding ring catching the light. He snaps and points at me. "Chicken sausage, you chickenshit."

Rocking back in my chair, I fold my hands over my

stomach and laugh out. "All I'm saying is it's hard to take you bastards seriously when you're on the news ringing the closing bell on the stock market."

"Contrary to what you think," Lydia says, sauntering into the room with Talent on her heels. "That's exactly why you should take them seriously."

Lydia Montgomery sucks all the warmth from the room, and I tug my collar away from my neck, finding it hard to breathe. Talent pulls her chair out and kisses the top of her head once she's seated, taking the spot beside her. She commands the space with perfect posture and grace—a queen on a throne. The rest of us are merely servants.

She sits marginally closer to Talent. Her hazel eyes check for his nearness, but his entire body gravitates toward her. He's stopped short by an invisible wall that keeps everyone at a distance, and he's looking for cracks.

How can he love her?

I can hardly stand to look at her.

And I definitely don't want to talk to her.

"Where's Camilla, Wild?" she asks, opening a copy of tonight's file folder to the first page. I haven't met Wilder's new wife Camilla, but I know she was one of Lydia's escorts before scoring the marriage proposal. Lydia herself was an escort until she inherited the kingdom.

The Ridge boys have a type.

"Sleeping," he says. He passes folders to Nicolai and me. "You mentioned having another one of your girls in tonight, so I didn't wake her up."

"That's good," Lydia says, fighting back a smile.

Shocks the hell out of me. The Ice Queen can actually smile.

The meeting begins with Talent and Wilder tag-teaming the contents of the portfolio. They start with the Coppola's legitimate investments. Nicolai and members of his extended family—cousins, uncles, nieces, and so on all have businesses in their names, for tax purposes. Nothing has thrown up red flags in the last thirty days, and his companies are growing at an impressive rate.

"Rip, this is something to consider," Wilder says, twirling a pen between his fingers. "We can create companies on your behalf unless there's something you have in mind. It can be anything. The paper trail is what's important. The last thing we need is the feds or the IRS snooping around your finances, and you're big time now. Big money. You're a very rich man, Alessi."

Snorting, I say, "I've been rich for a while."

"No," Talent interjects coldly. He circles a number on his own folder in black ink and slides it across the table. "You haven't. What you collected as a fixer was chump change compared to what you're worth now."

I keep my eyes pinned on the number. Not because it's more money than I can comprehend, and it nearly fucking is, but because if I look at him, he might see the truth in my eyes. And I'm not ready for that.

"This is what we have to lose," he continues, tapping his finger on the number. "And this is only the beginning. Continuing at this rate, we aim to double this in two years. Triple it in five. That money gives us the power to buy anything we want or need. Politicians, law enforcement, and the cooperation from the other families. Forget what you thought you knew before you stepped foot in this office, because this is a brand-new fucking day. This is the shit we talked about when we were younger, Rip."

As teenagers, we talked about the day when we'd inherit the family. It started out as something to be proud of. When we were a bunch of dummies with high ambition. But somewhere along the way, the focus turned to revenge. I don't know Talent like I used to, and I can't tell if he's being proud or vengeful now.

"Pray we keep showing up on magazine covers, chicken sausage." Wilder winks. "Ridge & Sons' success is directly tied to the organization."

"Who knows about this?" I ask, finding it difficult to wrap my head around how much the family is worth. There's a lot at stake. Others will want in. "We'll have targets on our backs."

Everyone is watching you. Waiting to see what kind of leader you are. California is a gold mine, Astore De Marco had said in Desolation.

"To be expected," Talent says dismissively. "Talk to Damage. Get a crew to keep an eye on the Cisneros. They're not stupid enough to make a move, but if they are, we'll deal with it. You're good at that."

"They think we're weak," I say, finally meeting his gray stare. "Anthony said we have something that belongs to them. He's gossiping like a fucking schoolgirl to The Ruin."

"Our worth says we're anything but weak," Wilder says. "What we're doing in Grand Haven is bigger than their gripes about a woman at our table or magazine covers."

"They're testing us," I say. "Allowing it to go unchecked is a mistake."

Talent closes his file folder. "We will not start a war with the Cisneros because their views on women in the workplace don't align with ours."

Lydia rolls her eyes.

"Does anyone know what they think we have?" Nico asks in a bored tone.

"A Cisneros doesn't have anything we want," Wilder says.

Agreeing with him is on the tip of my tongue when a flurry of activity outside the glass walls of the boardroom distracts me. I push my chair back, already reaching into my jacket for my guns when Vera walks into the office. The sight of her knocks the wind from my lungs like a punch to the stomach.

"Please, don't shoot my girls," Lydia deadpans.

Vera's cleaned up and pulled her hair back in a tight ponytail to expose the entirety of her neck I spent most of the day worshiping. Focused on balancing five glasses and a bottle of whiskey in her arms, she doesn't notice me and goes straight to Lydia.

"It sounds like you all need a drink." Her gaze sweeps around the table before finally landing on me. Inhaling a sharp breath, she drops a glass, and it shatters around the boots still on her feet, caked in drying dirt. "Shit," she whispers.

Everyone stands in aid, but it's Lydia who plucks broken shards from the floor and walks them to the trash can. "Take a seat, Vera."

Nico unscrews the top of the whiskey bottle and pours a finger in the remaining four glasses. "Yes, please, *bellissima*, have a drink with us."

"There're not enough glasses for everyone," Vera says, slowly regaining her composure. Uncertainty melts away and she's the girl on the pole under the red light.

"Have mine," I say, narrowing my eyes. "I don't drink."

Wilder snorts into his glass before throwing back a shot. "You still don't drink? You just live with it?"

"Live with what?" I ask. My eyes don't leave Vera.

"Your conscience."

A flash of anger crosses Vera's eyes, but she blinks it away. Lifting her chin in defiance, she announces, "Actually, I don't drink either. And I have some work to finish in Lydia's office, so enjoy."

We share a lingering look as she exits the room, and it doesn't go unnoticed by Talent. He leans back in his chair, resting his chin on his fist with a knowing smirk. But Vera's been living rent-free in the forefront of my mind for two weeks, and there's no vacancy for motherfuckers like Talent Ridge. Only, if he were not watching me so intently, I'd get up and follow her. Corner her. Trap her. Call her a fucking liar because I knew she had something to hide.

"She's one of your girls?" I ask Lydia, nodding toward the door Vera left from. "She dances for you?"

Lydia gathers the portfolios from the table and shoves them under her arm. "She doesn't dance for me. I don't own that club, and I don't know why she does it."

Because she's a dancer, I think to myself.

"She isn't only one of my girls, Rip." Lydia stands tall,

taller than any man in this room. Not in height, but in straight-up tenacity. I'm glad she's on our side. "Vera is the only girl who matters, Rip. She's the biggest moneymaker on my roster, she takes care of my high-profile clients, and she's tough. She's as tough as I am."

"I want her," Nico says, kissing the tips of his fingers. "Talent has you. Wilder has Camilla. I want Vera."

My trigger finger twitches.

My chest caves in.

Not because Vera is an escort. Not because she's the best Lydia has and I'm jealous. Nico wants her, so I can't have her. He's the only person I can't disobey. I took an oath. My life belongs to him. To this organization.

Some rules are meant to be broken.

But not this one.

Not this time.

Seven

Vera

Less than one percent of the world's population has violet eyes. It's actually an illusion. My eyes lack pigmentation. What looks purple is only light reflecting off blood vessels, but they're the first thing anyone notices about me. Followed by the size of my tits and the curve of my hips, but at thirteen years old, flat-chested and thin, the unique color of my eyes gave me value.

Human lives are spent like currency in organized crime. People are bought, sold, stolen, and traded for goods. My dad used me to settle his gambling debts with the Italian mob. The bargain was his daughter for his life. At least he had the decency to ask if I'd be well taken care of before handing me over.

Of course, anyone who accepts a living person as compensation has no integrity. He killed my father, and he kept me. The care lacked from the start.

"Take a look at my new toy," the man who'd acquired me announced to a roomful of people, squeezing my cheeks to move my head from side to side. *"Have you ever seen anything as remarkable as her eyes?"*

The loud pounding on my front door should scare me. I find it thrilling, instead, and relish in the sudden burst of heat running through my veins, warming my belly. Curling my bare toes against the hardwood floors, I squeeze my bottom lip between my teeth and watch the doorframe shutter like my bones. My stomach tightens with anticipation, and I hold my breath, waiting to see if the lock will give. Hoping it will.

He wants me bad enough to break the house down. Didn't take him for the romantic type.

No.

No.

That's not what his aggression means.

Unlearn that shit, Vera, I think to myself, forcing down a smile.

Aggression does not equal affection. I've read enough self-help books in the last year to recognize destructive behavior when I see it. This is nothing more than a temper tantrum from a tall, blond, green-eyed, muscular, sexy, well-endowed contract killer with a nice smile, who's been told no for the first time in his life.

I like it.

No, I don't.

The door is going to come off the hinges, and then who's going to pay to have it fixed? Me.

"Go away," I call out, crossing my arms over my chest. I tap my foot on the floor impatiently. Impatiently waiting for him to leave or impatiently waiting for the wood to fracture and break in a pile of shards at my feet? I don't really know. What I do know is that splinters are painful.

Say the door splits into sharp pieces. He'd be forced to

carry me to safety in his strong arms. Or spear me through the heart with the pointiest piece he can find. It can go either way. But I draw the line when the one-hundred-year-old windows start to shake. They do nothing to keep the heat in, but they're irreplaceable.

Storming across the foyer, I unlock the dead bolt and swing the door open. "What the hell do you—"

Fear is a jolt in the very bottom of my stomach and the breath caught in my throat. It's not as powerful as admiration, but I watch my face pale in the polished reflection on Rip's guns. Twin barrels are pointed right at my head, death close enough to kiss. He has his fingers on the triggers, the knuckles on his righthand tattooed with *Sink,* and the knuckles on his left tattooed with *Swim.*

"I should have let you fall," he says.

"You did," I answer, remembering our time on the roof. "This is the fall."

Silly rabbit.

Lifting my gaze to his, I dart my tongue out and lick the cool metal tip of his gun. Green eyes turn black when they're murderous, disks void of contrast and as empty as a killer's soul. But I watch them fill with color as he lowers his weapons, shoving them back into their holsters at his sides.

Rip Alessi drips testosterone.

He's straight-up male, rough and deep and torn. Uncontained and ill-mannered. He's a fucking barbarian. A Viking. A warrior. It makes me want to cry out, "Save me. Provide for me. Knock me up."

I'll be the fairer sex if he'll be my hero.

He's rolled the sleeves of his dress shirt up to his elbows, and the top buttons are undone. A light dusting of dark blond chest hair shows from beneath the fine fabric. Veins in his arms are full of blood, bluish under skin raised with goose bumps. I move forward to soothe them away, but he jerks his arm back and says, "You lied to me."

"Never," I whisper, momentarily distracted by his sharp jawline. Until I remember that he lied to me. "You said you weren't in the Mafia."

He lets out a breath. "I said I wasn't a hit man. I never said I wasn't in the Mafia."

Exactly.

This is a game of semantics.

"Underboss?" I shake my head. "That's a big deal."

He steps through the threshold into the house and slams the door behind him. I retreat. "Made men don't dish out information like that to normal people. But you're not normal, Vera. Are you? You're one of Lydia's fucking…"

"Say something disrespectful and I'll cut your tongue out." So much for being the fairer sex. I retreat, one slow step at a time. The back of my feet collide with the bottom stair leading to the second floor. I ask, "Does it bother you?"

Rip steps forward, pursuing me with a predator's grace. The goose bumps on his arms disappear under his shirt, and I know from experience that they reach his shoulders. I felt them under my fingertips this evening. "Does what bother me?"

"That I sleep with a different man every day?" I grip the banister, preparing to run.

His mouth curves into a devious smirk. There's nowhere for me to go but up, and he knows it. I'm trapped. "Not nearly as much as being lied to."

This should scare me too.

But he craves the chase, and I like to be hunted.

As he pounces, I spin around on the balls of my feet and take two steps at a time. It's a sad attempt to outrun a professional killer twice my size. Rip grabs my ankle, and I fall flat onto the flight of stairs. Kicking and screaming, I make a show of getting away, but my pussy is soaking wet and my inner muscles throb. He climbs over me, pinning me down as his hand comes around to cover my mouth.

Jerking my head back, he rests his forehead against my temple and says, "If I find out you're here to hurt my family, I'll kill you. No second thought. I'll eat your fucking heart out, do you understand me?"

Tears well in my eyes, even as I roll my hips to alleviate the ache between my thighs. He's hard against my bottom, as thick as I remember from our time in the woods. Over and over and over.

I shake my head, incapable of words. The steps press against my chest, crushing my diaphragm. They sink into my stomach and thighs, but this pain is nothing compared to the frustrating heat searing at my core. Sucking in short breaths through my nose, I turn my gaze to his and know he sees more than the dark purple this light gives my eyes. It's not fear, or reluctance, or shame looking back at him. It's recognition.

He lowers his hand from my mouth to my throat, and I moan.

"Jesus Christ," he mutters under his breath, standing straight and pulling me to my feet. Rip twists my arm around my back, and I cry out this time, but in excitement. Walking us upstairs, he asks, "What were you doing at Ridge & Sons?"

"Lydia called me right after you dropped me off," I say as he pushes me through the first door after the stairs. A guest room. Not that I've ever had a guest in my home. But it'll do. "She needed help with the schedule for the next few weeks. Camilla usually does it, but—"

Shoved forward, I hit the mattress on my hands and knees. The stupid decorative pillows I bought online in an attempt to be domesticated tumble on each side of the bed as Rip joins me from behind. He rakes his hands through my hair and tugs my head back.

"In the woods, you said it had been so long." His breath strokes the length of my neck, sending shivers down my spine. "But you're paid to fuck."

Backing into him, I rub against the proof that he wants me as much as I want him. "Not the same. That's not what this is."

He chuckles, pulling me up by my hair. I'm on my knees, and he holds me against his body. "No? That's not what this is? I'm not one of your fucking clients? Because I don't mind paying for it."

"That would be against the rules," I say with a smirk.

"Fight back, Vera," he growls in my ear. His hands slide up my top to my breasts, nipples hard under his palm. "Tell me to stop. Because once I'm inside of you, nothing or no one will be able to."

"Good," I whisper, dropping my head back to his shoulder.

Yeah, I think to myself, releasing a long breath as he slides into me. *Yeah, this is the fall.*

And I might die before impact.

The slow exhale ends with a short gasp as my body reminds me that I spent hours stretching it out in fresh ways.

Wonderful ways. Savory ways. Only two men had experienced me before Hush, and now dozens have been inside of me. Or maybe it's closer to hundreds of people at two thousand dollars an hour by now. But it was different with Rip today, like I'd saved parts of myself for him to shred and fill in.

He slams into me from behind, holding me tight around the middle with no give. Trapped in his arms, I'm left to absorb the momentum of his furious thrusts. The voice in the back of my head wondering if history is repeating itself, fades behind panting lungs and the collision of our bodies.

"You smell like me," Rip says. He throws his head back, releasing my middle to hold on to my hips. "There's still dirt under your nails and leaves in your hair. Like you could just wash me away when it was time to turn on for them."

Gripping the duvet, I tense as pressure builds between my legs.

Rip unravels my fingers from the bedding and tucks my arms in close. Using his knees, he brings my knees together and falls on top of me, crowding me, crushing me, covering every part of me with every part of himself as if I can be kept as a secret.

"Nico wants you," he says in a possessive tone.

"I know," I answer, quickly pushing away thoughts of the magnetic crime boss. He doesn't belong here.

Not now.

"He can't have you," he says more to himself than to me. His lips and teeth travel the length of my neck and shoulder. "You're mine. I've never wanted anything more in my life."

I nod. "Yours."

"Say it again."

"Yours," I whisper as my body comes undone. "I'm yours."

Later, when time swings somewhere between today and tomorrow, Rip and I drift somewhere between awake and asleep. His fingers sweep up and down my bare arm, from wrist to just above my elbow, before hesitating at an uneven patch of skin along my forearm. The break in momentum pushes sleep out of reach, and I turn in his arms, hiding my face against his side. He finds another scar on my back, and another on my shoulder.

They were there all along. He was too focused on what I'm hiding to see me clearly.

"Who did this to you?" he asks in the dark. I can't see his eyes, but I have no doubt they're as black as this room. "I'll fucking kill them."

Now that's what I like to hear.

Hush Series

Interested to read more about Rip and Vera, as well as the other characters in this story? Check out the book that started it all in the Hush Series now!

Tramp (Hush Volume 1)
https://amzn.to/3CWAXVj

Harlot (Hush Volume 2)
https://amzn.to/3oiK1jg

Criminal (Hush Volume 3)
https://amzn.to/3NXGRfs

Sign Up for my Newsletter!
http://eepurl.com/hxMAEX

About the Author

Mary Elizabeth finds words in chaos, writing stories about the skeletons hanging in your closets.

Known as The Realist, Mary was born and raised in Southern California. She is a wife, mother of four beautiful children, and dog tamer to one enthusiastic pit bull and a prissy Chihuahua. She's a hairstylist by day but contemporary fiction, new adult author by night. Mary can often be found finger twirling her hair and chewing on a stick of licorice while writing and rewriting a sentence over and over until it's perfect. She discovered her talent for tale-telling accidentally, but literature is in her choke hold. And she's not letting go until every story is told.

Follow me on Instagram.
Join my Facebook Reader Group.

"The heart is deceitful above all things and beyond cure."—
Jeremiah 17:9